5 - 111

WHAT READERS ARE SAYING . . .

"*Marvelous* is a fun mixture of suspense, teenage angst, love, and tragedy. It's a story that somehow hovers between hope and hopelessness. Travis Thrasher's stories feature characters that demand to be invested in and rooted for. He has a knack for crafting a story that leaves you wanting more, and thankfully *Marvelous* is definitely that type of story and a great beginning to a series."

TOM FARR

"*Marvelous* didn't just make me identify with a teenage boy; I *became* Brandon and felt his pain, loneliness, and joy. Thrasher's finely crafted thriller-mystery put my life on hold for a day, ruined my fingernails, and left me wondering how I could possibly wait until book number two."

CHRIS BAILEY PEARCE

"*Marvelous*, the first of the Books of Marvella, will draw you into a teenage world of pathetic parents, alcohol, drugs, bullies, outcasts, romance, mystery, and the supernatural. And it wouldn't be a Travis Thrasher story without a creepy uncle, a killer on the loose, corrupt police, and a classic rock playlist. Thank goodness it's fiction!"

BETTY JO HENDRICKSON

"Wow! *Marvelous* was compulsively readable; it hits a lot of the same notes that the Solitary Tales reached. If you like compelling characters with an intriguing premise, a bit of music, danger, and high school angst thrown in for good measure, all wrapped up in a story that explores themes of God's redemption—get ready. This first book hints at a series that is sure to be as wildly entertaining as it is unforgettable."

JOEL DAVIS

"Thrasher excels in making you feel what his characters are going through, whether or not you can personally relate. Only the best fiction can do that, and Thrasher does it so easily you barely notice until you start feeling along with the character. Thrasher is a writer unlike any other. He's written love stories, adventure, mystery, horror, Christian movie novelizations, and even a few extrapolations of country music songs. And he's good at them all. But creepy-YA-life-is-beyond-weird-coming-of-age stories? That's definitely what he's best at."

JOSH OLDS, LIFEISSTORY.COM

"Prepare to fall in love with a character who doesn't realize his own strength but keeps standing and fighting for the underdog anyway."

MELINDA BAUR

"Teen life is hard. Harder if you live with an abusive father in a dead-end town with a killer on the loose and a girlfriend with a dark secret. Travis Thrasher returns with *Marvelous* and sets the stage for the horrors to come."

JEFFREY KOTTHOFF, LO-FIDELITY RECORDS

"I am increasingly convinced that Travis Thrasher enjoys tormenting readers. He introduces his protagonists, inserts conflict along the way, and then—wouldn't you know it?—the book's ending leaves the reader hanging until the next one is released. As with Thrasher's previous series for young adults, the Solitary Tales, readers are going to finish the book and be ready to start the next one. I know I want to read the second in the Books of Marvella—*now!*"

KEVIN DENIS

"Fans of the Solitary Tales series have a wonderful new gift from Travis Thrasher. *Marvelous* introduces them to Brandon and Marvel, lots of mystery, an overarching sense of impending evil, and a love story that burns brightly despite numerous obstacles."

JOHN CLARK

"I just finished *Marvelous* and *wow*! I love it! Definitely written in classic Thrasher style, *Marvelous* is one book fans of the Solitary Tales will not want to miss. I love the town, the record store, the characters, everything. Brandon is such a selfless character, and Marvel is such a lovely enigma. I could not stop reading because I was totally enthralled with the story! I can't wait to see how things turn out in the series. I need more!"

JOJO SUTIS

"*Marvelous* is an amazing and uplifting feat of storytelling with real, believable characters you can't help caring about. This book—the entire series—is a must-read, not only for young adults, but for anyone who enjoys great writing."

DON BEARD

"'Remarkable' is one of the definitions of *marvelous*, and I think that the characters in this book have remarkable resilience. That's a trait that keeps readers interested in the story. There's so much heartbreak swirling around Brandon and Marvel, yet they are being pulled forward toward the plan God intended for them. Each time I read a portion, I was left thinking about the two of them. That is a sign of a good book."

JENNIFER CARTER

THE BOOKS *of* MARVELLA

MARVELOUS

TRAVIS THRASHER

THiNK

A TH1NK resource published by NavPress
e with Tyndale House Publishers, Inc.

NAVPRESS⏾®

NavPress is the publishing ministry of The Navigators, an international Christian organization and leader in personal spiritual development. NavPress is committed to helping people grow spiritually and enjoy lives of meaning and hope through personal and group resources that are biblically rooted, culturally relevant, and highly practical.

For more information, visit www.NavPress.com.

© 2014 by Travis Thrasher

A TH1NK resource published by NavPress in alliance with Tyndale House Publishers, Inc.

ISBN 978-1-61291-623-1

Cover design by Studiogearbox

Interior design by Dean H. Renninger

Some of the anecdotal illustrations in this book are true to life and are included with the permission of the persons involved. All other illustrations are composites of real situations, and any resemblance to people living or dead is coincidental.

Printed in the United States of America

19	18	17	16	15	14
6	5	4	3	2	1

THIS SERIES IS DEDICATED TO
MASTERPIECE MINISTRIES

MOSES ANSWERED GOD,

"BUT WHY ME?

WHAT MAKES YOU THINK
THAT I COULD EVER GO
TO PHARAOH AND LEAD
THE CHILDREN OF ISRAEL
OUT OF EGYPT?"

EXODUS 3:11, MSG

1

The worst feeling in the world is being stuck. Stuck in a place you know you can't leave, stuck in a position with no power. Stuck being a person you'd never trade places with.

Summer's barely begun, and I already feel like some kind of prisoner.

I walk past my brothers' bikes sprawled on the lawn, past the open garage that stands separate from our two-story house. I'm actually coming home with a piece of good news: I got a job at the record store downtown. But I don't find anyone inside to share it with. I grab a can of Coke from the fridge and glance at the stack of mail on the kitchen table—mostly unopened bills addressed to my father.

I wonder if and when I'm going to have to start helping pay some of those bills.

I hear the back door open and my brothers' excited voices. I step into the hallway and the first thing I see is blood on Alex's face and T-shirt. Carter is right behind him.

"Brandon, look at this," Alex says, holding one hand up to his nose. It's probably broken.

Not Alex, not now.

I know what happened, and I know that I finally have to act.

I rush back to the kitchen and grab a big butcher knife. No, that's crazy. I put it back and grab a big, round cast-iron skillet instead, holding it like a warrior about to go off to battle.

Alex has followed me into the kitchen and is still talking. "Carter's big head busted me on the nose," he says.

"What?" I stop and look at him again. My heart is racing. "What were you guys doing?"

"Wrestling on the trampoline."

I sigh and let out a tidal wave of anger.

"I didn't mean to," Carter says. "What are you doing with that frying pan?"

I shake my head and put the skillet away. Not that I would've done anything with it anyway. It was just an impulse.

Carter laughs and runs off to the family room.

I poke my head into the room and see my father in his usual place on his armchair throne, eyes focused on ESPN. "I got another job," I tell him.

He nods and looks at me the way he always does. Like I'm some kind of stranger. At least I'm not a stranger holding a cast-iron skillet, prepared to whack the side of his square face.

"Who would hire you?" Carter asks, and laughs at his own joke. "Someone whose grass you cut?"

Carter's a little full of himself. Comes from being the baby, I guess, and Mom and Dad's obvious favorite.

"At least someone around here has a job," I say.

"Carter's not the one who busted up his car, is he?" Dad says.

He's just trying to irritate me. I don't say anything, because I can't deny it. I do have a busted-up car. Which is exactly why I now have two jobs this summer.

I turn to head upstairs to my room.

"You need to get your crap out of the garage, 'cause I'm cleaning it out."

"Okay," I call back.

I'm asking for trouble by not saying "Yes, sir," but I'm already halfway up the stairs so I get away with it. It's a ridiculous request anyway. My father "cleans the garage" at least once a month. It's just an excuse for him to hide out and drink the day away while claiming to Mom that he's working on something: his car, a washing machine he hopes to sell, the motor from a dishwasher. Things that have been broken since forever.

When I'm upstairs and Alex passes by me again, I shake my head. "Change your shirt," I tell him.

For a second he wonders what I'm talking about. "Oh, yeah."

Four males in this house. Sometimes it's not a pretty sight.

Mom's running late at the law office where she works as a paralegal, and I'm doing anything I can to stay clear of Dad. I pump air into the tires on my bike, since it will be my main mode of transportation this summer. I have an older bike in the garage too, one that I've said is garbage but Dad keeps saying he'll fix up and sell. If I had a dollar for every time he's said one thing and done something else, I could buy a new car. A really nice one.

Dad's an electrician, or was, till he lost his job—he hasn't electrified anything in years. Work got scarce when the housing market tanked years ago, and during my sophomore year it dried up altogether. Dad's mood went from slightly overcast to pitch-black.

"Got the bike out, huh?" Dad walks by me and I freeze. For a second he looks down at my bike, then he keeps going to the back of the garage where his work table sits. There's a big Chicago Bears flag behind it, along with pictures of the 1985 Bears. The wonderful, infamous '85 Bears. There's a funny shot of William "The Fridge" Perry doing a touchdown dance.

It's a bit sad when you know your father loves a 325-pound defensive lineman from several decades ago more than his own son.

"So—you gonna go find a third job?" Dad says, his back turned to me. "Since they're so easy to get?"

I don't respond, because I'm not sure where this is coming from. He's the one who told me I needed the second job because I'm paying off my car—the car that got crashed by a friend.

Dad turns around and looks at me. "You think you know what it takes to be the man of the house?" he asks.

I think of those bills again. "No, sir."

He nods slowly, then smiles. It's the meanest sort of smile I've ever seen. The kind the bad guy flashes right before he beats the hero to a pulp.

Maybe I need that skillet after all.

"You guys just stay so busy with your jobs. . . ." His voice fades out as if he's talking to himself.

I just stand there, not sure what to do, really unsure where this is going. I'm not even sure who he's referring to. Mom and me?

Dad snaps out of whatever it is. "Go on inside, okay?"

There's not one bit of hesitation in me. I don't need to understand anything. I don't need to ask what's happening with him. All I want to do is get out of here.

Back inside the house, I feel a little better. Mom will be back from work any minute with her clueless, busy self, and that'll make me feel even better. But something's going on inside Dad that can't be explained by a couple of beers in the middle of the afternoon. This—this whatever it is—scares me.

It scares me because summer has only begun. And Dad has nowhere to be except here. Maybe I *should* get a third job.

2

"Brandon?"

The voice whispering my name seems to come from some-where in the sky. I think I might be flying, but I don't ever really remember my dreams. The only thing I see in the dark-ness is my digital clock declaring that it's almost 2:00 a.m.

"Brandon?"

It's Alex. He shares a room with Carter across the hall.

"Yeah."

"Did you hear them arguing?"

Even though I'm still trying to wake up, I know who he's referring to.

"No. When?"

"Just now."

Alex is whispering in a way that sounds like he just ran around the house five times before rushing up to my room.

"Why are you out of breath?"

"Mom was crying."

I suddenly realize my brother is totally scared. "I'm sure everything is going to be fine," I tell him.

I might have my own doubts about this, but I'm not lying. I wouldn't lie to my brothers. *Everything will be fine if I have anything to do with it.*

"Do you think they're getting a divorce or something?"

Now I know what's going on. It's because the Swansons down the road—neighbors we've known forever—are getting a divorce.

"No, that's not going to happen," I say.

"Isn't that why Dad went out to see you in the garage?"

"No. He was just checking on me."

"You sure?"

"They're not divorcing. Who knows what Mom was crying about. She's probably just tired. It's two, you know."

"Yeah."

"Go back to sleep."

"Okay," he says.

"Did Carter hear?"

"You can't wake the dead." Alex isn't trying to be funny. He's being honest. Carter sleeps like an unconscious person.

"Okay, sorry to wake you," Alex says.

I want to tell him more. A lot more. I want to explain how there's no way Dad is leaving Mom, simply because he has no other family who would take him in. And since he has no job, there's nothing he could do and nowhere he could live. Dad's not leaving this house.

As for Mom, she won't leave Dad. She puts up with his drinking with a nice dose of denial and a bit of *he'll get better once he gets a job.* There's a side to Dad she doesn't see, that my brothers don't see. I think of Alex's frantic breathing and realize I'm happy to be the only person who sees that side of Dad. I guess that's the responsibility of being the oldest brother. I'll take it. For them, I'll take it.

I wish I could tell Alex to just go to bed and dream of a paradise to come. To imagine some kind of wonderful place where dreams come true and people live forever and happiness is a real thing. Some kind of really awesome place. But like I said, I don't lie to my brothers.

3

It's only been two weeks, and I'm already tired of my second job. Or maybe I'm just tired because the storms kept me up last night. Usually I'm a sound sleeper, but a loud clap of thunder woke me up and I couldn't go back to sleep. That's why my head is throbbing this morning and why I'm a little more out of breath riding my bike to work. And maybe that's why when I see two guys beating up some poor kid at the bike park, something snaps inside me.

There's nothing I hate more than bullies.

Nobody else is around. When it's sunny out, the parking lot next to the park is usually crowded. But though the rain has stopped for now, the clouds are still thick and there are puddles everywhere. I see a bike lying in the grass not far from where the fight is taking place.

The bigger of the two guys doing the beating is yelling something and kicking the kid, driving his shoe into his side and his back. I'm surprised not to hear any sort of screaming or crying. I park my bike next to the other one.

When I get closer I recognize both the guys. Football players. Meaty, thick-necked jocks. Just two of the many reasons I never bothered trying out for the team. Greg Packard, the big guy in black sweats trying to pick up the kid by his T-shirt, is going to be a senior this fall, like me. The tanned kid next to him is Sergio. Who they're beating up is a mystery.

I see a baseball bat on the grass nearby and snatch it up just as Sergio turns toward me with a look on his face that says he thinks I'm there to help them pummel the guy. Greg calls the kid a name and tells him to get back up. For a second I see an angry face looking up in defiance. His nose is bleeding.

"You little creepo, get up—"

These are the last words Greg says before I swing the bat against his leg, the same leg that was kicking the kid on the ground. I expect Greg to go down immediately. Instead, he screams in pain and turns around. I guess I should've hit harder.

"What the—" He leans over and grabs his thigh, cursing. Then he recognizes me, calls my name, and curses again.

The kid on the ground pulls his T-shirt together and starts to sit up.

"What are you guys doing?" I ask, the bat still nice and firm in my hand.

"We're showing Seth Belcher here what happens when you flip off strangers."

The name doesn't sound familiar. The guy stands and wipes blood off his upper lip. He's taller than I thought he'd be.

"Are you okay?" I ask him.

Seth nods and accidentally smears blood over his face. He doesn't look okay.

"Give me that bat," Greg says.

"Are you guys just bored when you're not hitting people?"

Sergio stands there looking at me, but Greg lunges. I swing the bat again and hit his arm. My swing doesn't have a lot of power behind it, but it still stops him.

"You are stupid, you know that, Brandon?"

"If you come near me again, I'll crack this thing over your head. Not that it'll do any good."

Seth walks toward his bike.

"What's this have to do with you?" Greg asks. The rage I see in his face looks familiar. Once again, something inside me, something like a switch, goes on.

"Two guys are beating up someone a lot smaller than them. And kicking him when he's on the ground."

"You're next," Greg says.

"I know who your father is. Don't tell me he'll put up with this," I say.

Greg's father is a cop, and I know Greg is about two breaths away from being kicked off the football team for good.

"Give me my bat," he says.

"It's the only thing preventing you from jumping me right now. I think I'll just keep it for a little while."

He shouts an obscenity. "You know, I'd break your face if I wanted to."

"I know where you live," I tell Greg.

"And I know where *you* live," he says back. "It really sucks to be you, doesn't it? What's it like living with that drunk daddy of yours?"

His words shock me. Greg must know about my father's run-in with the cops.

But there's no way he knows the full truth.

I toss the bat on the ground and walk slowly back to my bike. Seth is already pedaling away. I guess he's saving his thanks for a sunnier day.

Greg calls out another colorful four-letter word as I leave. I'm not afraid of him. If he wants to come after me, let him. Let him get kicked off the team and ruin his senior year. I'll keep standing.

I've learned by now what it takes.

4

It's just after noon, and the store has been dead all morning. Harry Reeves, the owner and manager, is cranking up a best-of album by a band called Siouxsie and the Banshees. One of Harry's pet peeves is when his employees don't know the music that's playing; twice I've gotten nailed for having no clue. Now I always make sure I know, just in case a customer says, "Uh, hey, who's this?"

I see the girl the moment she walks into the store. She wears a wide-brim hat that hides most of her dark hair. She glances at me, then looks around as if she's expecting someone else. A lot of the customers at Fascination Street Records are regulars, but I know I've never seen her before. She's wearing a yellow short-sleeved top, a long skirt with bright flowers on it, and boots, like she's dressed up for a fancy party and someone gave her the wrong address. Maybe the wrong decade.

For a moment I look down at the counter and act like I'm doing something, but she still walks over to me. Cheerful eyes the color of a chocolate bar stare me down.

"Hi, I'm looking for Harry. Are you him?"

I shake my head. "No, he's around somewhere."

"Okay." She looks behind me at the shelves of unique collectibles and rarities that Harry keeps behind the counter.

"Can I help you?"

She opens a retro purse as colorful as her dress and produces a red piece of paper that looks familiar. "It says there's a job opening for a 'friendly and inquisitive soul,'" she says, reading the paper.

It's the same ad I was clutching when I walked in here a couple of weeks ago. The job I had to beg Harry to give me, even though I'm not Mr. Sparkling Friendly and I'm not really that inquisitive.

Don't tell her that, you tool.

"Oh, yeah. He's still looking for that."

I'm not sure why I just lied.

"I can wait," the girl says.

I glance at the back door and remember Harry told me he was driving to St. Charles to meet a guy selling his vinyl collection. That's only about fifteen minutes from Appleton.

"You ever worked at a record store before?" I ask.

This was the first question Harry asked me.

"No."

And the same reply I gave him.

"Why should I hire you then?" I ask, still repeating the conversation that got me hired.

"Are you the one I'm supposed to talk to?"

I nod. "Yeah, that'd be cool with Harry."

Maybe it's the fact that I stood up to those jocks that's

giving me an air of invincibility. Though inside I know there's no way Harry's going to hire someone else.

"I'm friendly," she says with a smile. Not the kind of smile I used to get from my ex-girlfriend Taryn, the kind that says I'm-all-that-and-more. This really is a friendly smile.

And hot, too.

She's a mixture of a sweet, dark-eyed girl plus a bit of a South American model thing.

"Do you know a lot about music?" I ask.

"I do, in fact. And don't stereotype—I listen to more than Latino music." She says something in Spanish, and I suddenly wish I hadn't gotten a C in it last year.

"Sorry, I didn't quite apply myself in Spanish class."

"I said my favorite artist is Stevie Nicks. Can't you tell?"

I nod, but I have no idea who Stevie Nicks is or why I should be able to tell.

"Wait a minute," the girl says in disbelief. Friendly disbelief. "You don't know who Stevie Nicks is? Come on."

"Don't tell Harry. Especially if she's from the eighties. He's got a thing for the eighties."

"The hat? The dress? Totally seventies. Have you ever heard of Fleetwood Mac?"

"Of course."

"Oh, sorry, don't let me insult you."

Suddenly, I've become a lot more friendly and a whole lot more inquisitive.

You're hired.

"Okay, so you pass the music and fashion test," I tell her. I look more like a soccer player, which I am, than a rocker. But that's okay—Harry doesn't care what I wear.

"Do I need to fill out a job application or anything?"

Yeah, give me your cell number and address.

"What days can you work?" I ask. I'm digging myself deeper and deeper.

"Any days but Sundays," she says.

"We're not open Sundays."

"Well, that's good then."

"Nights okay?"

"Well, I do have a curfew, but yes, nights are okay."

I can't tell if she's joking, but I don't ask. The bell signals an opening door, and I glance over to see if it's Harry. I don't want him to come in and tell her the truth.

"Do you have any other jobs?" I ask. *And also, do you have any boyfriends or big brothers?*

"No. But I might have to get another job, depending on the hours here."

If I don't hurry up, she'll realize that Harry has zero hours to offer her. "Okay, well, yeah, you seem to fit the position well," I say.

For a moment she remains silent and smiles. I wonder if she knows I'm full of it. Finally she says, "That's it?"

"Yeah, sure."

"So what's the pay?"

"Oh, it's $9.50 an hour. Does that work for you?"

She nods, the smile still there.

"Can you show up tomorrow? At noon?" Of course I'm working tomorrow, but I'll figure it out by then.

"That sounds great. There's just one little concern."

"What's that?" I ask.

"Do you need to know my name?"

I laugh. "Nah, we don't use those around here. Yeah, sure."

She extends her hand and I shake it. "It's Marvella, but everybody calls me Marvel."

Why, yes. Of course they do.

"Nice to meet you, Marvel."

Very nice to meet you.

5

The closest I get to telling Harry about Marvel is just before I head home at nine thirty, half an hour after the store closes.

"Hey, Harry—you like Stevie Nicks?"

He's passing by with an armful of records and says a quick "Sure." I just stand there, knowing I'm not going to tell him what I've done.

Harry's a cool guy. This record store has been around almost ten years now, and I know it doesn't make a lot of money. I know 'cause he's told me so, but not in a *My-life-is-utter-misery* sort of way. He's got a funny attitude the same way he's got funny, curly hair. "Keep the faith," he says, and then laughs and plays some music.

"You need anything before I go?" I ask him.

"Sure, you want to babysit three boys?" He's got a two- and a four- and a six-year-old. He says lately he's been walking around terrified because it's that time again. The two-year itch, he calls it.

"I don't think you'd want me babysitting," I tell him.

"I don't think you'd survive it if you tried." He laughs at his own joke.

I want to tell him I hired someone and she's starting tomorrow, but I don't know how. If I'd been smart enough to get Marvel's number I could call her and tell her the truth, but nah, I didn't do that either.

Somehow I need to figure out how to get through tomorrow without being embarrassed *or* getting fired. I realize that it'd be worse to be fired. I still have my car to pay off. The car that got totaled by one of my best friends, Barton Menke, when I wasn't even there.

Barton should've graduated this past spring, but it didn't turn out that way. He had hoped to basically not study his entire senior year of high school, and someone like Barton has to study. He's just not that smart. Then again, how smart was I, letting him drive my car after an end-of-the-year party?

It was a good thing he hadn't been drinking. That was one of the reasons Barton was driving. In fact, none of the guys in the car were partyers. They were just fans of El Burrito Loco and thought it would be a great idea to get burritos at midnight. I was tired and went home to bed. Big mistake that turned out to be.

The Nissan Altima wasn't *that* great of a car. I bought it for $8,000 since it was about five years old and had a lot of mileage on it. I paid $4,000 and my parents paid the other half. Well, Mom paid, with my assurance I'd pay them back. Dad wasn't too happy about the arrangement in the first place, and when he heard about the accident, he had a whole faceful of *I told you so.* He said I needed to pay them for the car by the end of the summer. Which gave me a whole heart-ful of *Thanks so very much.*

The accident happened on a side road near El Burrito Loco. A road crew had blocked off half the street, because about a hundred yards of it had been turned into an eight-foot-deep pit. Guess what Barton did? He found the only pos-sible way to sneak through the barriers, then drove down the road, only to slide off into the hole. He didn't blast off and kill himself and the others. But he saw the hole coming and tried to avoid it, toppling the car over and totally warping its frame. The tires were busted and the sides were mangled, and the insurance guy said we might as well buy a new car. Since, yeah, insurance wasn't going to pay me anything.

Barton told me he'd pay for it. I seriously doubted I'd see the money anytime soon. The guy was already in hot water with his parents for being forced to repeat his senior year, so they weren't about to bail him out. And he still didn't have a summer job, while I had two.

I leave the record store and hop on my bike, and in two seconds I realize the obvious. The tires have been slashed.

I don't need to wonder who did this.

I mean, yeah, sure, maybe Marvel figured out I was bluff-ing and opened up her switchblade. But I'm seriously think-ing it was Greg and Sergio.

I'm also thinking that stuff between me and them has only just begun.

Devon picks me up in his brand-new Jeep Wrangler. It's shiny and red, and his parents gave it to him on his birthday last spring. I got twenty bucks, and Devon got a new car. Life's not fair, but I've known this for a long time. At least I can call him to pick me up after I've pushed my bike to a shop a couple of blocks away from the record store.

"How's the record business?" Devon asks.

"I met a girl named Marvel."

"Sounds like a comic," Devon says. "Or a comic book, not a comic, since I doubt she's a comedian, right?"

Devon Teed's mind is a little like a shotgun. Each thought is a blast in a different direction. Sometimes he's talking with you, then you realize he's talking to himself. Sometimes you forget you were even talking to begin with, because you're fascinated with listening to Devon.

"She's pretty hot," I tell him. "A Hispanic girl, seems pretty cool."

"Can she talk English?"

I shake my head. "No, not at all. Except to ask me if I want a flour or corn tortilla."

Devon doesn't mean to sound arrogant or racist. He's just dumb sometimes, simply because he's lived a white, white life. There really is a white picket fence around his house, and his mother still helps him put sunscreen on his pasty skin.

I don't tell Devon about hiring Marvel. He'd have a lot of fun at my expense with that one.

"So who's this kid you got your bike tires slashed for?" he asks.

"Seth Belcher. Know him?"

Devon thinks for a moment. "That guy is weird."

"He's quiet."

"No, he's weird. I remember him in ninth grade talking about a cat he killed."

I laugh. "I hate cats."

"Yeah, but you don't go around killing them."

"Well, I don't go around beating kids up either. Those guys are punks."

"That Greg is a psycho," Devon tells me. "Watch out for him."

"He keeps it up, I'm going to his father."

Devon pulls into his driveway and shuts off the car. I hear the crickets in the background. Devon looks at me with a serious gaze.

"Don't get him kicked off the football team. They need him next year."

"If he gets kicked off it's 'cause he's an idiot."

"You're an idiot messin' around with him. That's all I have to say."

I laugh because I know Devon will have plenty more to say.

"And don't even get me started about Sergio."

Yep. Devon always has more to say.

We spend a couple of hours playing on his Xbox, till his mother invites me to stay for dinner, as she always does. I'm sorta the adopted son around here, since Devon is an only child. I get more love in the Teed household than in my own. I'd tell my father this too, if I thought it would change anything.

I realized long ago that you can't do anything about your place in this life. Like being the oldest kid in our house, for instance. I'll never know what it's like to be spoiled like Carter and Alex. Dad tells me I was spoiled once too, but I don't think so. The first kid gets treated like a grown-up way too soon.

Devon offers me a ride home, but I tell him I'll walk. It's only a couple of blocks, and it's safe in Appleton, even at ten at night. I head home on the familiar sidewalk, crossing a street and stopping to look at the clear sky. Tonight the stars are extra bright, and I wonder what it would be like to be up there with them. To be looking down instead of up.

I like being outside at night all alone, even if it's just a short trip like this. Back to the house and whatever it might bring.

For a moment I think of Marvella. Or Marvel. I wonder if she's going to be at Appleton High School next year, and if she really is as cool as she seems. I wonder what she'll think when I tell her the truth about the record store. Maybe I can work something out with Harry. Or maybe things will crash and burn like they did with Barton and my car.

A lot of life is out of your control. People like Dad want to think they are in control, but really nobody controls anything. You wake up one day and find your car totaled. Then a couple of weeks later you wake up and something marvelous walks into your life.

In both cases, you didn't have a single thing to do with it.

The house is silent, and thankfully Dad is sleeping. So even though things are out of my control, I do what I can. I can come home late hoping to avoid drama. I can sneak inside and make it to my room without any headache. I can try to sleep and think about the girl I'm going to see tomorrow morning. I can dream about the things I'd like to say to her. I can try my best and then hope.

When my best doesn't work and my hope fades, I can fight back.

Harry is cool about me keeping my own hours. He tells me the days he'd like me to be here and asks that I put in at least six hours or so. Today I'm earlier than usual because I have something to tell him.

He's leaning over the counter sipping his coffee as usual. Some new alternative band is playing in the background, and I remind myself to see what he's playing. He might be in the mood for some of his favorites from the eighties, then he'll suddenly spring something on me like the latest album by a hot band. Harry's not a music snob. He just loves music.

After stalling for ten minutes I get up my courage and go over to him. "Hey, can I talk to you?"

He looks up. Today he's wearing his thin, rectangular glasses. He has three different pairs that he changes up just like he does his music. "What's up?"

"I wanted to ask about maybe hiring someone."

For a second he just looks at me. "What do you mean?"

"Like hiring someone new."

"Are you quitting?"

"No."

"Good. I need you."

"Maybe you need someone else, too."

"We've already got Phil. 'Course you know him."

Phil is our resident hippie. I'm not even sure if he gets paid to work. He mainly chats it up with townsfolk and hangs out when there are live music events in the store. Most of his comments sound like quotes.

"But what about maybe *thinking* about hiring someone else?"

Harry shakes his head and takes another sip from his coffee mug. "We're all good here."

The phone on the wall behind him interrupts us. It's an old-school phone with a really loud, obnoxious ring. He picks up the receiver, the cord dangling all the way to the floor. He got the longest phone cord he could find so he can roam around the store holding the receiver. I asked him once why he didn't just get a cordless, and he said he liked phones attached to something.

I sigh and am about to wander off when I hear him say a loud "What?" and then follow it up with a "Yeah, I'll come now." I think there must be a crisis at home.

He's already around the counter when I turn to ask what's going on.

"Stay here, okay?"

"Everything okay?"

"No. It's—there's an emergency by the river."

"Your family?"

"No," he says. "Thank God. Louis Kramer said they found a body in the river. He knows I used to be an EMT and I'm just down the street."

His whole demeanor has changed. This is superhero Harry. Maybe he has a secret identity like Batman. Businessman record-store owner by day; dark, slightly overweight knight after sunset.

"I'll be back in a short while. Man the fort."

The last time he left me in charge I hired the first pretty girl to come in. Who knows what might happen today.

She walks in wearing flared jeans with a funky brown belt and a short-sleeved rainbow top and matching knit hat. Her dark brown hair covers her face on both sides as if she's peering out from behind blinds.

"Hello, Brandon," she says. "Isn't it a beautiful day outside?"

"It's hot." Just like I've suddenly become.

"So is the owner in?"

"He just ran out for some reason. An emergency."

"Really? Does he have curly hair, glasses?"

"That's him."

"He was running down the sidewalk and bumped into me. I could tell he felt awful."

"Yeah."

"I love when things like that happen. Meeting people before you're officially introduced. Or running into people at odd times. It's cool when God orchestrates stuff like that." She says this in a perfectly natural way as she picks up an album on the counter. "This looks like a fun album."

Marvel stands and waits for me to tell her what to do.
I almost tell her the truth. About her not really having a job
and all that. But I can't. I don't know why. Girls don't make
me stammer. I can tell anybody anything. I can do it in front
of everyone, too, just like I did with Taryn. But something
about Marvel makes me pause.

"What made you want to work here?" I ask. "Besides seeing the job listing."

Her face lights up. Like there's a spotlight suddenly shining on it. "*That* is a long story. Well, not exactly long, but
I would need to put it into context. So . . . let's just say I'm
meant to be here."

I nod.

Maybe you are.

"Okay. Let's get to work."

As in "let us," both of us. And even though the "us" might
be incredibly short-lived, I'm glad to be able to say it now.
Before Harry comes back and ruins everything.

Thirty minutes later, the phone annoys me again. I pick it up
and hear Harry, sounding out of breath.

"What's going on?" I ask.

"They found a kid in the river."

"Is he okay?"

"No. He's dead. Cops and firemen and paramedics were
out here. It was a mob scene."

"Where?"

"Right under the bridge. It was—" He lets out a deep
breath. "It wasn't pretty."

"Who is it?"

"They don't know yet. He couldn't be identified. Just—seriously, it was bad. We just know he's some teen. It was awful."

"Are you still there?" I ask.

"Yeah. Just give me a little while."

"Okay." *No rush.*

"Man, some parents are about to receive like the worst news ever. And I don't even want to know how he died."

"You think he drowned?"

"No. No way. He was dead long before he hit the river."

"How do you know?"

There's a pause. "Look—just stay there. I'll be back in a while. Thanks."

I get off the phone and see Marvel looking at me.

"Someone drowned?"

For a second I don't respond. I'm not sure how to.

"What happened?" she asks.

For the first time since I met her, I see a different look come over Marvel's face. It's fear. And it's not just mild, curious fear.

She looks terrified.

8

The bell rings as the door opens, and Harry walks in. He shuffles down the short flight of stairs into the cavernous store. I've been waiting on him for a while, having set Marvel to work unpacking boxes in the back. I get to Harry quickly.

"Look, I don't know anything more than what I already told you," he says.

"Harry—I need to tell you something."

"What? You know something about the kid in the river?"

"No. No, nothing about that. I hired someone."

He stops and looks at me. The new album by the National is playing through the speakers surrounding us.

"I can't hire anybody. I told you."

I've come up with a plan. "Look, she's already working. I'm training her."

"Are you crazy?"

I nod. "Give her the job."

"And fire you?"

"No, don't fire me." I look back for a minute to make sure Marvel's still in the back. "Just don't pay me."

"Why would I do that? Are you high or something?"

Then I see his expression change, and I turn to see Marvel entering the room. It takes Harry about a millisecond to figure out the deal.

"Hi, are you Harry?" she says as she walks up to him and shakes his hand.

"No, I'm the guy who plows over girls on sidewalks."

"I'm Marvel."

Harry thinks this scene is funny. "Brandon's told me all about you."

I nod and raise my eyebrows. I know Harry could ruin this in a single moment.

"I love your store. It's very hip."

"Well, you look pretty hip yourself, so I take that as a compliment. We need all the help we can get, don't we, Brandon?"

I nod and wait for him to say more. But Marvel asks him a question.

"I probably need to fill out some forms, don't I?"

"Let me show you in the back," Harry says. "The IRS really likes to have their info, so yeah, you'll need to fill out some stuff. I'll go over everything, since—well, sometimes I don't trust Brandon."

I give him a *thank you* smile and he just shakes his head in a way that says *Boys*. I'm not sure how this is going to play out exactly, working for someone and not getting paid. But maybe Harry will have compassion and maybe I'll win the lottery and maybe it'll all pay off when Marvel falls crazy in love with me.

For now I'll be happy to go on a date. Not that I'd be able to pay for anything, but I'll figure that out later.

About half an hour later, after Harry has gone over some things with his new employee, he finds me in the *S* section of vinyl.

"Do you know a kid named Artie Duncan?" he asks.

I nod. He graduated from Appleton High last spring.

"I just got a text—that's the kid they found by the river."

"Artie?"

I can see him walking down the hallway laughing with his buddies. He's the kind of guy everybody likes, friends with the jocks and the party crowd and all the other crowds.

"He's dead?"

"Yeah. Don't say anything. His family's been contacted, but it's not public just yet. They go to our church. His mom's gonna have a rough time."

I don't know what to say or how to act.

"Look—you good about showing Marvel everything?"

"Yeah."

Harry looks at me. "We'll talk about that later. For now, I gotta get home and tell my wife. She's friends with Nancy Duncan. I won't be long."

He's been gone about ten minutes when Marvel comes out from the back office. "What's going on?"

"They found a guy I went to school with down at the river. Dead."

"What do you think happened?" Marvel asks.

"I don't know. Harry doesn't think he just drowned. It's kinda creepy."

"Do you know—did he believe in God?"

I shrug at the odd question. "Harry says the family goes to his church. So that's a good sign."

That doesn't seem to make Marvel look less anxious.

"Nice day to start work, huh?"

"Harry didn't seem to have any idea I was coming." Her eyes are wide and bright underneath the knit cap perfectly positioned on her head.

"He's just disorganized like that. So, you said your family moved."

"Yeah. From Chicago."

"Why'd you move to the suburbs?"

"I actually moved in with my aunt and uncle."

"Oh, really? How come?"

"Because I had to."

This is the sort of answer my father might give me when I ask him something. *Dad, why do I need to pay you guys the full amount of the car by the end of the summer?* He'd say because he told me so. Or "Just because."

I decide not to press Marvel about the reason she's living here. "So what year are you?" I ask.

Nobody has come into the store and probably nobody will, at least not until later this afternoon.

"I'll be a senior," Marvel says. "Attending Appleton."

"That's where I go."

"That's what I sorta guessed." She says this in a playful way, not a sarcastic make-me-feel-like-an-idiot sort of way. "Do you like it?"

"Yeah. Except for some of the guys on the football team. And some of the girls."

"You don't play sports?"

"I play soccer. Of course, nobody really cares about that." *Especially my father.*

"You lived here your whole life?" she asks me.

"Yeah. Nothing's ever happened like a guy getting killed. This town is quiet. Quiet and boring."

"Quiet and boring can be good sometimes."

"Says who?" I ask.

"Someone coming from a loud, crazy, out-of-control world."

There's a lot more to this statement, just like there's a lot more to Marvel. But I don't ask. Maybe in time I'll understand what she's talking about, and where she's from, and why quiet and boring is a good thing.

Then again, if she prefers quiet and boring, maybe I have a chance.

9

Where are you guys?

Barton. I read the text and roll my eyes. It's eight o'clock, and Frankie and I are at Devon's house, watching TV in the basement. Barton would've probably been here too if he hadn't wrecked my car like an idiot.

I just checked out the quarry but nobody's there, he texts again.

Some of us are working for a living, I text back.

You're not working I already checked at the record store!

I don't text him back, so I get another buzz on my smartphone.

I already have $500 to give you.

Then you'll only owe me $3,500. I'm not being nice, because I know Barton. He'll put it off and eventually forget to pay me.

What do you guys think about Artie???!!! This is why he's texting. It's all we've been talking about for the last hour, though nobody knows anything more than we did when the news first broke. **My dad talked to Mike Harden about it.**

Harden is one of the only Appleton cops I know by name, besides Greg Packard's father. He's spoken at our school before and is a good enough guy.

Come on where are you guys??

I know he's trying to get an invite to hang out with us again. **We're at Devon's**, I type back.

Cool. I'll be there shortly. I gotta ride my bike everywhere.

Thank God, I type.

"I heard his face was all cut up like paper strips."

Barton's only been here for five minutes and I'm already regretting it.

"Sick," Frankie says.

Frankie's one of my best friends, the quarterback at our school and the greatest guy I've ever known. He's a far better athlete than he gives himself credit for, which is why I, along with the rest of Appleton High, love him. In my dreams I'm catching the winning pass from him in the final seconds of the final game of our final year of high school. But soccer players don't touch the ball, and in my case I probably couldn't even if I tried.

"How would you know this?" Devon asks him.

"Sergeant Harden said so."

"Oh, what, he personally called you and told you this?"

Devon and Barton look funny side by side—the tall, lanky guy and the short, chubby guy. Add the good-looking black football star to the mix, and my friends are quite the odd bunch.

"He told my father," Barton says, a little defensively.

"And what? Were you in the pantry spying on your parents?" I joke.

"I overheard enough. And then I asked my dad later. Are your parents freaked out about it? Mine sure are."

"My mom is paranoid," Devon says.

"I haven't been home yet to ask them about it," I say.

"No doubt about it, he was murdered," Barton says.

"You don't know this," I say.

Barton shakes his head. "Man, just wait."

"Just wait for what?"

"The end of the world as we know it." Barton says this in a mocking, *muwahaha* voice. The other guys tell him to shut up.

This is the gang of four, the same group since freshmen year. Barton latched onto us that year even though he was a sophomore. I think a lot of the guys in his class were tired of his jokes and humor (and lately I can see why). We're a mix of jock, nerd, crazy guy, and me. I'm not sure what category I belong in. In some ways I'm sorta like an Artie Duncan. A kid who gets along with most everybody. Except his father and the two morons beating up a poor kid in the park.

I tell Frankie and Barton about the bullying I saw and how I hit Greg Packard in the leg with a baseball bat.

"Greg? And Sergio? Are you crazy?" Frankie says.

"They were totally beating some kid's butt."

"Who?"

"A skinny kid named Seth."

"Seth Belcher?" Barton says. "What a turd."

"You know him?" I ask.

"He's a weirdo. He's always got his headphones on."

"You don't want to mess with those guys," Frankie tells me. "They already cut the tires on my bike."

"Did they have a beef with Artie?" Barton says.

We all groan. He says so many inappropriate things that *he's* gonna be the one beat up one day.

"I'm just saying. You don't know."

"Greg and Sergio are thugs, but they're not murderers," Frankie says.

"How do you know who's a murderer until they actually get caught?" Barton says. "I mean, everybody thought that man who had the girls locked up in his house was a pretty nice guy too. Some guy used to have cookouts with him. Then they find girls chained up in his house."

"Are you trying to tell us something?" I ask, trying to lighten the conversation.

"I'm trying to tell you that something bad's coming. People are scared. A guy our age just got killed. Who knows who's next."

We're all quiet and suddenly very bummed.

"It's nice to have you come hang out," I joke.

Barton just nods.

I hope he's wrong. Very, very wrong.

The first thing I do when I get home is check on my brothers. Usually I'm hoping they're not around to annoy me, but tonight is different. I find them upstairs in the spare bedroom we've converted to a game room, with a couch we got from our uncle and an entertainment center with a flat-screen television and several gaming systems.

"Where're Mom and Dad?" I ask. I sit on the chair in the corner facing the two of them on the couch.

"Mom went to bed and Dad's passed out in the basement," Alex says.

Alex is fifteen, and in spite of being three years older than Carter, he's the smallest of all of us. He seems so easily breakable—one of the many reasons I feel a need to stand up to Dad.

Carter ignores me and keeps playing the game. He's a goofball, a good-looking, athletic kid. Always been easygoing, likable, popular. He's Mom and Dad's favorite, and they've never even tried to hide it.

"You guys hear about the dead boy they found?"

"Mom's freaked," Alex says.

Carter just laughs and bobs his head.

"Did you know him? The guy who drowned?" Alex asks.

Oh, you mean the guy whose face was cut up into little paper strips?

"A little."

"What do you think happened?"

"I don't know."

"The news says they're investigating, that it could be a murder."

I look at Alex and just shake my head, trying to get him to be quiet in front of Carter.

"I know everything that happened," Carter says.

I have to remember that he isn't six anymore, even though he sometimes acts like it.

"Did Mom and Dad say much about it?"

"Dad was acting really weird tonight," Carter says. He's

still staring at the screen, killing soldiers and making blood go everywhere.

I try to get Alex to tell me what that means.

"He was in a fabulous mood tonight and decided to drink extra lots," Alex says with his typical sarcastic tone.

For a second I feel a sick sensation inside of me. Then I hear the knock on the door and I literally jerk. Mom opens the door, and I let out the breath I was holding.

"Are you okay?"

"Yeah, I'm fine," I tell her. "Why wouldn't I be? I texted you where I was."

"I want you coming home early from now on," she says.

"Mom, look—"

"No. They're saying Artie Duncan was murdered. We don't need you riding your bike around in the middle of the night."

"I was just over at Devon's."

"Then you can have him over here," she says. "Your father and I discussed this."

"I'll be careful," I say. "For all of us."

She knows this means I'll be looking out for Alex and Carter. That's what big brothers do. Especially when those brothers don't have a father looking out for them.

But the thought of having to spend evenings at home dealing with my dad is worse t   han having to ride my bike around with a possible killer hiding in the woods.

Sometimes you can lock the doors and close the blinds, but the monsters are still there inside your house, sleeping and breathing and just waiting to wake up and terrorize you all over again.

10

Before heading to my other job of cutting lawns, I sit down at my laptop and search Facebook for Marvel's name. I know that her last name is Garcia, so I look up a variety of names she might go under. Marvel, Marvella, even Marv. Nothing comes up. I do, however, see something strange on Frankie's page. It's a picture of someone whose house has been majorly TPed. All the trees in the yard are raining toilet paper.

The picture's been shared on Frankie's page, which is generally pretty inactive, so he probably doesn't even know it's there. It's from someone I don't know who's tagged about a hundred people. Then I see what's written next to the photo: *Second time this poor guy's house has been TPed in the last year. What did Seth Belcher do to anybody?*

I take another look at the names of the people tagged and recognize a bunch of them as football players.

I'm pretty sure I know who did this. As sure as I am about who slashed my bike tires.

I'm cutting the grass when a truck stops on the street and the driver simply watches me. At least it seems like I'm being watched.

Don't become Mom.

I'm not someone who jumps at horror movies or wakes up in the middle of the night with nightmares (that would be Alex). But ever since hearing about Artie Duncan, I can't help being a little cautious. Artie wasn't some loner, and he wasn't a wimp. The day before he showed up dead, he was home with his parents and everything was fine in his life as far as anybody knew. If he really was murdered, then it makes sense for anybody in Appleton to be a little cautious. Especially when an old Chevy Silverado is just sitting there on the curb of the lawn I'm cutting.

I stop the mower and look back at the truck. Because of the brightness of the day, I can't see inside the cabin. And with my wide sunglasses, the person inside can't tell if I'm for sure looking at him. So I guess it's a standoff.

Don't become Artie Duncan.

The truck moves away with a groan. I'm sure it's nothing. I'm sure it has nothing to do with Artie.

But maybe that's what he thought too, until someone offered him some candy and he took it as a joke.

The summer has just started, but somehow I feel it's going to be different from any other summer I've ever had.

I arrive at Fascination Street about fifteen minutes before Marvel is scheduled to show up to work. I'm supposed to be "training" her this week, so that means I'll be working with her every shift. I already cut two lawns this morning, and now I'm at the job with no paycheck attached. But I'll figure out something. I'm pretty good at that.

There's an older guy with long hair looking at the Led Zeppelin shirts. We attract several different groups here at the store. Hippies like this guy. The alternative crowd, a group which to be honest I can't exactly sum up, since it's so varied. It could be a guy in all black who is a skater, or could be a girl with purple hair and five nose rings. Then there are the kids who have too much free time on their hands, the ones who come into the store because they want to buy the new Vampire Weekend album on vinyl. They look like Vampire Weekend and talk about Vampire Weekend and I really wish they'd just go away.

Harry must be depressed or something today, because he's playing an old album by a band called Clan of Xymox, which should be subtitled The Saddest Group in the History of the World. I'm waiting for Marvel and checking my iPhone when the music stops and the lights go out. There are windows on two sides of the shop, but since the store is sunk down into the ground it's never totally bright. The T-shirt guy doesn't react, just keeps looking at shirts as the lights flicker back on, then off again, then on. The slow, moody music starts up again, stops, and starts up again like a death drone.

The power comes back on just as Marvel walks through the door. She smiles as she sees me looking at her with what is surely a weird look on my face.

"What's wrong?" she asks.

"Did you see that? Or feel that?"

"Feel what?"

"The power just went out. Like, just went out for a second." *And then you walked in and turned it back on.*

"I didn't see any storm clouds in the sky," she says as she puts her purse behind the counter.

She smells like strawberries and looks like a fashion model in a loose-fitting yellow dress that comes to her knees. It has a flowery, lacy sort of top. She's as tall as me in her high platform heels.

"Like your outfit."

"I found this in a store for five bucks," she says, gesturing to the dress.

I half expect her to spin around in it. Then I realize I'm standing there staring at her while she waits for me to tell her what to do. "Let me go get Harry," I say. *Let me dunk my head in some cold water too.*

I'm seriously not usually like this, even with the girls I've liked in the past. Maybe it's because things ended so badly with Taryn. Maybe it's because I already have that summertime itch where I'm wishing it was the school year again. Or maybe it's just the effect Marvel has on me.

Harry comes out and puts on an album by the Cars. Seems like he can't play that depressing stuff with Marvel around. "Brandon here has donated his time specifically to help train you," he says, knowing he's teasing me.

"I'm here to help," I say.

Harry lets out a laugh. Soon T-shirt guy buys three black ones that all look the same. I show Marvel how to ring him up. A monkey could do this job.

For the next hour I show her how to stock and organize and restock and keep track of inventory, and I know it's way too much detail for anyone to absorb in one afternoon. As I'm talking, I'm thinking of the things I really want to say.

Do you have a boyfriend?

Are you interested in going out on a date?

What do you like to do in your spare time?

But soon she asks a question that makes these others go away. "Did you hear any more details about the boy who was killed?"

I shake my head. "I saw a couple of articles online. Nothing new."

"What are they saying?"

"That it was a pretty sick way for someone to die. He was cut up really bad. Missing parts of his skin. Something out of a horror movie."

"That's awful."

"Sorry," I quickly say. "Don't mean to freak you out."

"I'm not freaked out. I'm just sad. Sad that the world is so evil."

"Stuff like this happens in Chicago, not Appleton."

"It happens everywhere," Marvel says matter-of-factly. "You can't keep evil in a cage. It roams around like a wild beast. It can follow you anywhere. Anywhere."

She walks away, and I'm left with goose bumps as the Cars play over the speakers. "I guess you're just what I needed. . . ."

Just what I needed. Yes indeed.

11

"I'm dozing off watching you kill people."

Devon spends as much time playing video games as I do working. And it shows, since I'm on the couch next to him falling asleep while his character in the game refuses to die.

"It's late anyway," I say.

He pauses the game and looks over at me. "I need to tell you something."

"You're starting to get arthritis in your hand?"

Devon doesn't laugh, and that means he's deep in thought. I really hope he's not going to start talking about another Fear Zone video game releasing this summer.

"It's something Artie Duncan told me once."

I look at him and know he's not joking, but I still expect a punch line. "What?"

"About Otis Sykes."

"I didn't know you hung out with Artie."

Devon shakes his head. "I didn't. He was my lab partner in geology one semester. We were talking about stuff—oil drilling, fracking—then we got onto the subject of Sykes Quarry."

Appleton's quarry is named after Otis Sykes, a reclusive older guy I've never seen, only heard of.

"So what did he say?" I ask.

"To stay away from that guy. From Otis Sykes. I asked if he knew him, and he said yeah. He said it in a way that was like a definite 'Yeah, totally know the guy, and I'm afraid.'"

"So what are you saying?"

"Nothing. Just . . . Artie said that last semester."

"Have you told anybody else?"

"No, 'cause, well, I don't know. It's probably just something he said. I'd forgotten about it till yesterday. But . . . you know?"

"People have been talking about creepy Otis since I was a kid," I say. "But I've never even seen him."

"Me neither."

"Maybe we don't *want* to see him."

"Maybe," Devon says.

He's thinking way too much, which can be a scary thing. I'm too tired to talk about it.

Doesn't every town have a cranky old guy that kids make up stories about?

A couple of nights later, a whole week after Artie Duncan was found dead in the Fox River, I get a text from Devon as I'm closing up the record store by myself. I'm a bit cranky because I was expecting Marvel would be working with me. Some guy came in and kept me late, talking about how music was getting louder these days but quality was going down. I really,

really wanted to find something interesting in the conversation, but I couldn't. Still, I was nice and pleasant so Harry wouldn't fire me.

Devon's text reads **Meet me by the quarry. Seriously.**

Sykes Quarry is not far from the record store; I can take a bike path and cut through the woods to get to it. There is a massive swimming pool with a beach around it, a place that stays busy through the hot summers. The guys and I go there sometimes, though it tends to attract more families and screaming kids than hot girls.

Why? I type back.

Going to the quarry during the day is one thing, but I have no idea why he wants to go there tonight. It's almost ten and the quarry is closed.

'Cause if I disappear tonight you're going to feel guilty when I show up dead.

For a second I laugh, but then remember our conversation the other night and I'm not sure Devon is trying to be funny. **Where are you?**

Come on the bike trail and you'll spot me.

I tell him I'm leaving in a few minutes. Sure, the police and parents and adults everywhere have been warning us for the last week not to stay out at night and not to be alone and not to do a lot of things. But I don't know. The bike path still seems safer than other places. Plus, I'm very curious.

The path eventually links to a dirt drive that circles around to Sykes Quarry. There's a chain-link fence at the edge, where you can look down and see the quarry. It's less to keep people out than to prevent a car or bike from driving off the steep incline. I coast on my bike until I hear someone calling my name.

"You took forever," Devon says.

"I was closing down the shop. You could've come in and helped."

He's dressed in black, and his forehead and his cheeks have black on them.

"What's all over your face?"

"Camo."

I take a sniff. "Smells like shoe polish."

"Never mind. Leave your bike up here."

"Where are we going?"

"Just come with me."

I follow him down the road to the entrance of the quarry, but Devon doesn't go inside. Instead he heads toward a field that leads to the parking lot. The sky is overcast, so we don't stand out too much walking around here.

"What are you going to show me?"

"Something I spotted the other day and didn't have the guts to stick around and investigate further."

This really doesn't inspire confidence, but I follow him anyway. He leads me beyond the empty lot and toward the woods. Devon seems to know where he's going. I follow him into the trees and up a steep hill.

We walk for about ten minutes. It's too dark in these woods to tell if we're on a trail or not. About halfway up the hill, Devon stops and puts a finger on his lips. He points to my right.

There's a house in the woods. One little light is on outside a door.

"I didn't know there was a house here."

"Shhh," Devon says again. "Just listen."

We stand there for what feels like an hour. At first I'm intrigued, but when nothing happens I get bored. I'm about to say *What are we doing here?* when I finally hear something. It's a low rumbling sound. Like an engine of some kind.

"What is that?" I ask.

Devon only nods and raises his eyebrows.

"Seriously, Devon, what was that?"

"That's Otis Sykes's house."

"Sykes? Quarry Sykes? Lives *there?*"

"You're a genius," Devon says in a hushed voice.

We hear a door opening, and both of us drop to the ground. Then we hear footsteps, followed by the sound of someone digging. If it wasn't late at night and I wasn't holding my breath feeling my heart beating in my mouth, I'd say *no way* to any of this happening. But it is.

I start to say something, but Devon cups a hand over my mouth. The digging continues for a little while, then the shuffling sounds again and the door closes. Soon the light goes off.

There's no more engine rumbling. Devon eventually makes a gesture that we should go. I've been ready for the last half hour.

"What was *that* all about?"

It's fifteen minutes later, and I've followed Devon back home. We nearly got spotted by a cop, but managed to get off our bikes and duck into some bushes as he drove past the path. It's not like we're breaking the law, but we've been highly encouraged not to be out at night. The last thing I need is a cop telling my parents to keep me in after dark.

"So what's this all about?" I ask. "What made you decide to become a detective?"

Devon is all hyper energy at the moment. He goes and checks to see if his parents are anywhere near, then proceeds to break out a candy bar. "There's something I have to tell you," he whispers. "Something you can't tell anybody."

This surprises me. I thought I knew everything about Devon. "What?"

"Just hear me out, okay?"

"Okay . . ."

He looks around again to make sure the coast is clear before he speaks. "I bought pot from Artie. A few times."

I laugh. I can't help it, but I do. The thought of Devon buying drugs. Or smoking weed. It's crazy. "Shut up," I say.

"And what I think—I think he used to get the stuff from Otis. Or maybe from a guy who got it from Otis."

I add everything up in my head even as Devon keeps talking.

"I wanted to see if Otis Sykes lived around here. Because of what Artie said."

"So you went *looking* for him in the middle of the night? Hoping to find—what? More pot? A drug lord?"

"I went the other night with Barton."

"What?" I ask. "He knows about this too? Where was he tonight?"

"He's as loud as a rhinoceros. The other night he kept laughing."

"Were you guys smoking then?"

Devon doesn't answer, which is a yes. There's something both amusing and creepy about this. Amusing because I've never even seen Devon drunk. Creepy because what if the drugs had something to do with Artie's death?

"That engine," I say. "What's that about?"

"Maybe he's cooking drugs. Like meth or something."

"You've watched too much *Breaking Bad.*"

"A kid got killed. A guy who deals drugs. The cops are eventually going to find that out."

"So this Otis guy—was that him? Did you see him? How old is he anyway?"

"I asked my parents and they don't know. Old. Old enough, I guess."

"Why's he digging in the middle of the night?" I ask.

"Maybe he doesn't want to be spotted digging during the day. Maybe it's a drug transaction."

This is all a little too much for me. "Don't you think we should tell someone else? Like the cops?"

Devon just shakes his head. "I don't want to get into trouble. Even if it has nothing to do with Artie, I think there's something going on there. Something really weird."

"Yeah. You smoking pot and spying on old dudes."

Devon doesn't laugh. He looks as serious as I've ever seen him. "Don't you think the quarry has had a weird little vibe going on around it for some time?" he asks. "With the guy it's named after?"

"Not really."

"Remember the summer they found all those dead birds here?"

I shake my head. "You think they were killed and sacrificed to the evil Lord Sykes?"

"Just wait and see," Devon says.

"Wait and see what?"

"I don't know. But that's my point."

I think Devon has too much time on his hands. That along with an imagination fueled by comic books and video games.

I have something else fueling me. Or I should say, someone else.

12

I can't sleep. I'm thinking about what Devon said about Sykes and the quarry. I'm not sure if the guy has anything to do with Artie's death, even *if* Sykes was supplying pot to him. Every show I've ever seen about killers ends up revealing that it's the guy living right next to you, the one who smiles all the time and helps you with your groceries and takes care of your cat and will also slit your throat in the middle of the night. I watch a lot of late-night crime television. I know these things.

Appleton is just like a lot of other towns west of Chicago. I've lived here my whole life, in this suburb of about 23,000 people. It's not as affluent as the nearby towns of Geneva and St. Charles, but it also is a lot more upscale than a place like Aurora. It's got different pockets inside it. A pocket of old, small houses, especially near the downtown area. Then it's got an area of really large, sprawling mansions. There's a newer shopping area and an old, somewhat abandoned area. It's a town that talks a lot about growth and change but hasn't really grown or changed much at all. Some of the people, especially the old-timers, fight change.

Near downtown the river splits in two, creating on one side a small, bay-like circular area where the water sits surrounded by sidewalk and buildings. They call it the Riverwalk, and a lot of different functions take place there. I've always dreamt of getting a Jet Ski and taking it out into the small bay, but I don't even know whether that's legal.

There are three massive old churches near the downtown area, and all three are empty. One is used for town hall meetings and stuff like that. Another is supposed to be torn down. The third is due to be restored.

The downtown area is small, with a lot of empty shops and office spaces. Every now and then a new store pops up, but very few make it. So many people go to large thoroughfares like Randall Road to do all their shopping. It's a minor miracle to even have a Wendy's or a Target near downtown.

Fascination Street Records just seems to fit Appleton. It would seem odd in a place like Geneva, with all its fancy little stores for grandmas who love to shop. But people who love vinyl make special trips to Fascination.

A portion of downtown called Rush Street was recently renovated, with brick and stone and even an arch over the entrance to the street. Some restaurants and shops are there, and they're trying to do something new. My mother loves how it looks, but Dad says it was a waste of money.

My parents have never really been involved much with this town. Occasionally my father goes insane about something new happening. He especially vented when they moved Binny's Beverage Depot out of town. God forbid they take away his favorite store and the source of all his meanness.

There are maybe half a dozen Appleton residents I can think of—most of them old—who are just plain odd. But then again, doesn't every town have that?

Appleton is no different from anywhere else.

Who knows what really happened with Artie, or whether the killer is even from this town? He probably comes from sweet little St. Charles. Maybe he runs a flower shop and sells cute little bonnets to old ladies and their granddaughters in their nice Sunday dresses. Or maybe it's that novelist who lives on the Fox River in Geneva and writes all those scary novels. Who knows?

All I know is that there are weirdos everywhere. Artie dying has everybody spooked. I don't want to join them. There's no reason I should.

"Oh, great."

Marvel is standing by the window watching the rain fall, and she looks back at me. "What?"

"Summer rain sucks," I say.

"Why? I love days like today."

"Some of us don't have cars to drive around in."

"I don't either," she tells me.

"At least you have someone picking you up."

She already knows my whole bike saga. I told her to gain sympathy, but she just said I shouldn't have let Barton take my keys. She sounded like my parents.

"I love really hot days when it's raining," she says, looking back outside. "You can stand in the middle of a street and let the drops fall on you and feel refreshed. It's like God's little sprinkler."

I'm getting used to these sorts of statements, taking something I never thought of and turning it on its head. I was just complaining about having to ride my bike in the rain.

Marvel walks back over to the counter where I'm sitting. Harry is off doing something, since we have the store quite well under control. He still hasn't figured out what he's going to do with me. He's paying Marvel, just as I had hoped. And somehow, my schedule keeps lining up with hers.

"It is nice to get a short little rainstorm when you're playing ball."

"Are you talking about soccer?" she asks.

"Oh, no—I'm talking about when I shoot basketball with the guys. I'm not that great."

"So, soccer, basketball . . . do you play football?"

I smile and shake my head. Somehow she's managed to find one of the touchiest subjects in my life.

"Why not?" Marvel asks. "You look athletic enough."

"Oh, yeah, sure. Like a big defensive lineman."

"No. I was thinking more of a quarterback."

I nod and glance at the droplets falling outside the window right above the counter.

"What?" she asks. I imagine my expression isn't the happiest.

"My father was a quarterback," I say. "He used to dream of me being one too."

"You don't like football?"

"I don't like my father."

Her dark eyes don't move off of me. I feel strangely close to her, talking in the middle of the rainstorm here. I feel comfortable sharing stuff like this, stuff I'd never say to anybody else.

"Sorry," she says.

"It's fine. Typical family drama."

"No, I'm sorry for bringing the football thing up."

"It's fine. I decided a long time ago to play soccer. I really love it. And I really love how it infuriates my father."

"Have you ever tried an opposite approach?"

This is funny. Marvel has no clue who she's talking about.

"No."

"I think our parents—or whatever adults we're with—are put there for a reason. Despite all their flaws."

"Some have more than others," I tell Marvel.

"My father tried really hard, but he was gone all the time," Marvel says. "I tried to accept that and not resent him. But he just—I think he just got lost."

"So what's your relationship like now?"

"He died."

"Oh. I'm sorry."

"You didn't know," she says.

I feel like a fool, having talked about my hatred of my father in front of a girl who lost hers.

"That nice-looking black guy who came in the other day. Frankie? That's your friend, right?"

I nod. Suddenly I feel a bit jealous.

"You said he played football."

"QB," I tell her. "Now *he's* a football player."

"Maybe you can take some lessons."

I shake my head. "That ship passed. Or sailed. Or whatever you say. It's fine. A lot of the football players are morons anyway."

"Morons need people to lead them," Marvel says.

"That's why they have Frankie. But nah—I'd just be another moron."

"You're a good guy, Brandon."

This comes out of nowhere, but it feels so natural. It's sweet, yet it also makes me feel about ten and Marvel about twenty-two. I smile at her but don't say anything more. I'm not sure what to say. I'm not sure she's right.

13

I half expect Marvel to offer me a ride home, but she doesn't. She doesn't even tell me who's picking her up tonight. We talk about everything, but then again, there are things she doesn't talk about at all. Like her aunt and uncle and pretty much anything about her family. I'm not going to ask. I'll wait. In time she'll tell me, just like she told me her father had died.

I don't want to say the obvious, but it's there, deep down. I know it before I even think it. *Maybe my father should join him.*

I shouldn't think this, but I do anyway. It's the truth.

I close the shop door and make sure it's locked, then I go to unlock my wet bike. Before I reach the bike rack, I see the lights of a car suddenly turn on and hear the engine rev up.

"Get in."

Speak of the dead.

It's my father in our Chevy Malibu. He's here to pick me up. I'm far more terrified than I was last night spying on the creepy recluse. "I can ride home," I tell him through his open window. "It's not raining too hard."

Any harder would be a downpour.

"Get in. Now."

I move around the car and do as I'm told.

Once inside, I know what's up. I can smell Dad, and I know bad things are about to happen. "I need to get my bike," I tell him.

"Leave it there and get it tomorrow." His voice confirms that he is drunk. Not sorta drunk like he always is, but real drunk. The kind that results in blackouts and black eyes.

"Really, I can get it."

He grabs my forearm and squeezes it as hard as he can. Dad is strong, and even stronger when he's like this. The pain tears through me.

"Just shut your mouth. Leave your bike there. It's your fault you don't have your car anyway."

There was a time in my life when I wanted to know what was wrong with my dad and what had happened and how I could try to fix it, but I know better now. Something is always wrong and something always happened and nothing can fix it. Except perhaps death by hanging.

"Your mother gave me the whole guilt treatment when I told her I wasn't going to pick you up. So here I am. After stopping for a drink on the way. Aren't you happy?"

"I didn't ask to be picked—"

He slaps my head with the palm of his hand. "Just shut up. I'm already tired of listening to you. You know how whiny you sound?"

Dad curses, and I wonder how else he can be a bad

example. For a moment, I close my eyes and picture Marvel. I think of her smile and her dark eyes. I wish I were sitting beside her instead of here.

I keep quiet, and there's no more drama. My arm hurts from being gripped so hard, and my head aches from being swatted. But as we get to the driveway, I realize I'm almost in the clear. *He's tired. An hour earlier might have been worse. But he's tired.*

I see Dad's eyes close, and then I help turn the steering wheel into the driveway. This nudges him awake. He jerks the car to a stop and waits for me to get out. I don't hesitate. Then I hear the car squealing behind me and peeling off down the road.

I hope he crashes into a tree. Maybe, possibly, somehow I'll end up regretting that thought. But right now I really do wish he'd die. And I don't feel an ounce of regret saying so.

"Brandon?"

I want to just say hi to Mom and keep her from asking any questions. Most of the time I can do that in the busyness before school and work or the tiredness afterward. But I can tell she's in the kitchen waiting to talk to me.

"Did your father pick you up?"

I nod. "Yeah."

"Did he leave?"

I nod. The hardest thing about this conversation is not thinking of something to say, but holding back the things I want to utter out loud. Like *Do you really not realize you're sending a drunk man out to pick up your son?*

"I just didn't want you getting soaked," Mom tells me in the shadows of the dimly lit kitchen.

And maybe I didn't want to be slapped like some fly.

"Did he tell you where he was going?"

"No." *But I have a feeling he's going to drink a little more and then maybe pass out somewhere.*

She waits. Without the canister lights on, I can't see the deep wrinkles around her eyes. Hopefully she can't see I'm on the verge of screaming at her.

"How was work?" she asks.

"Fine." *A lot better than the ride home.*

Maybe Mom is worried and wondering, but I don't know. She's seen Dad angry, of course, and heard him lash out, but he's always saved the choice words and body blows for our one-on-one sessions. Mom probably figures I'd tell her if there was anything worse, something that crossed a line. But for now, I take the hits and keep my mouth shut. *You've got enough to worry about without knowing Dad likes to beat up on his son.*

"I'm so tired," Mom says.

There's nothing left to say. This is a typical Mom-and-me conversation. I can get away with saying little, because Mom expects that. She assumes boys are just that way. And maybe they are. But I'm only silent because I don't want to awaken a living nightmare in her home.

I hang out with my brothers for a while, but all the time I'm thinking of Marvel. I wish I had her number. Not that she'd necessarily want to talk to me, especially since we talk all day long, but who knows? Maybe I'll ask for it next time I see her. Or maybe I'll ask her out. Maybe I'll even do both.

14

Whenever I have a lawn to mow that's not nearby, our neighbor Glyn lets me borrow his truck. I don't know what he does, since he always seems to be home. Maybe he's like Dad and lost his job. The difference is Glyn hasn't lost his grip on life. He's got three trucks, and he's always been cool about loaning me the beater to pull my trailer around. He's offered to sell it to me, but why would I buy it when he's willing to let me borrow it for free? Now, instead of owning two vehicles, I have none and am working to pay off the one I once had.

It's a sunny morning as I head out to do a couple of lawns before going to work at Fascination Street. I'm driving on a side street a couple of blocks away from downtown Appleton when I see a tall figure walking on the sidewalk. He's all in black, from his cargo pants to his band T-shirt. His hair is straight and long, grazing his eyes. I almost pass him by before I realize it's the kid I saved from getting his butt beat.

I stop and roll down the window of the passenger seat. "Hey, you need a lift?"

When he looks at me, I see that he's not quite *all* in black—he's wearing a white Japanese headband with the red dot in the middle and Japanese writing on it. I want to laugh because I wasn't expecting that, but I catch myself.

"No." His voice is really low and doesn't fit his skinny form. I wonder if he recognizes me.

"I'm Brandon—we didn't have a chance to talk. I'm the guy with the baseball bat."

"Yeah, I know."

Well, so much for thanks. "Those guys been messing with you anymore?"

"I can handle it."

I nod.

Okay then.

"Well, look, it's Seth, right?"

He nods.

"Let me know if you need anything, okay?"

"Like what?"

I shrug.

Okay, fine, three strikes and you're out.

"Take care," I say and drive away. I hate it when I try to be nice and get attitude in response.

"They brought someone in for questioning about Artie Duncan," Devon tells me on the cell phone.

"According to who?"

I've just showered and am about ready to go to the record store and sweep Marvel off her feet.

"Barton."

"He should be a spy or something."

"They brought the person in yesterday. So who knows."

"Do you know who it is?"

"Some guy."

"Well, of course it's some guy."

Usually killers don't end up being middle-aged mothers or young women. Seems a lot of times it's ordinary guys, those you don't pay too much attention to. Not a loner guy like a grown-up version of Seth. And not the weird guy living by himself in the woods. No, usually it's an under-the-radar guy. The one nobody really knows until he's famous and you learn he kept body parts in his freezer.

You don't need to go see a scary movie anymore to be freaked out. All you have to do is hear about something on the news and Google it to find out the sick results. The Internet is full of horror stories.

"What if it's someone we know?" Devon asks. "Like some teacher? Like Mr. Midkiff?"

"Mr. Midkiff a killer?" I laugh. "Come on." Midkiff is our science teacher who graduated with a master's in dorkdom.

"You know how the vein pops up in his forehead when he's angry?" Devon says. "I'm tellin' you, it could be him."

"I gotta go."

"What are you doing after work?"

"Hopefully hanging out with the hot girl I work with."

"Really? I'll have to drop by and see this girl."

"Sure. Anytime."

"Maybe I'll have to ask her out."

We both know this is a joke. Devon doesn't ask girls out. He hasn't had the best sort of luck with the ladies.

"Maybe," I say.

"I'm going to find out more about who they interrogated," Devon says.

"You've watched too many detective shows."

"It's better to be on the lookout than to have someone looking out to kidnap you."

I laugh. "Nobody would kidnap you. You'd talk them to death."

"That's not nice."

"It's true."

"Yeah, maybe."

"See ya later."

Before I have a chance to figure out how to get around to asking Marvel out today, she asks if she can talk to me for a moment. Outside the building.

"What's wrong?" I ask.

She's wearing a cream-colored beret that once again looks like nothing I've seen. The girls at Appleton High aren't going to know what to do with Marvel.

"I'll tell you outside. I don't want to talk here."

Harry is around, so I tell her sure and open the door for her. We go around the side of the record store to the narrow parking lot. My bike is locked up next to the brick building.

"Brandon, I've already told you this, but I think you're a nice guy."

Oh, no. Not this line. Not this conversation.

"I just can't get involved with anybody right now."

"Wow," I say.

"What?"

"I just got dumped and we weren't even dating."

She laughs. "I'm not 'dumping' you. I'm just being honest."

"Okay."

"Look, I'm not sure how often you work, but I do find it sorta interesting that you're always working the exact same hours I am."

I smile. "What a weird coincidence."

"Yeah. Crazy. Especially since we're *so* busy."

I nod and look at a car passing by on the street slightly above us. Cool graffiti art lines the wall of the building next to us.

"So let me ask this, hypothetically speaking," I say. "Let's say I asked you to go out sometime."

"No. See, that's what I'm talking about. I told you. I can't get involved right now."

"*Involved* is such a technical word."

"What word would you like me to use?" she asks.

"I don't want you to use any word."

"And I don't want you to ask me out."

The sun feels warm on my face. I squint as I look at her. "How come?" I ask.

We're no longer speaking in hypothetical terms.

"Because I just can't."

"You couldn't, for instance, have pizza with me down the street one evening after work? What's the difference between talking there and talking here?"

"This is my job. I'm paid to work here."

I'm not.

"You don't seem to mind talking to me," I tell her.

She moves a lock of hair that is floating in front of her eyes. "I can explain someday, but not now."

"There's someone else," I say.

"No."

"You just broke up and you're not wanting to date for a while."

"No."

"You're engaged to some rich Saudi Arabian guy you'll marry after you graduate high school."

She laughs. "Yes, how did you know? I can't believe my secret's out."

"It's pizza. That's all."

"It's not *just* pizza. It's complicated. *I* am complicated, Brandon."

I smile and nod. "I know. That's why it's such a good idea."

And why I haven't given up, even though the signs all point to my needing to give up. I'm not usually like this. In fact, I've never been like this.

"I'm sorry," she says. "I will explain more. It's just—I don't want you to think I'm crazy just yet."

"I already think you're a little crazy."

"A little?"

I nod. "That's a compliment."

"Okay, then. Thank you. You're a nice guy."

"Stop right there. Enough with this nice guy stuff. *That's* why things are complicated. If I was a bad-boy rebel hunk dude it wouldn't be that complicated, now would it?"

"Well, no, of course not. If you put it like that. A bad-boy rebel what again?"

"Hunk dude."

"*That* is exactly the sort of person I'm looking for in my life now. And I'm sure that's why God wanted me to start working here."

"Oh, God brought you to Fascination Street, huh?"

Her look is suddenly different. Still smiling, but this time not as playful. "Yes, he did. That's why things are complicated. And that's why . . . We should go back in, okay?"

I notice a couple of shoppers have gone inside the store. I nod and follow her back in.

My interest has suddenly just quadrupled.

I say a very casual and a bit distant good-bye to Marvel as she leaves. Then when the door shuts, I realize how it sounded. I realize that even though there's no way I want to act like that, I'm starting to give her some attitude. Because she said no before I could ask and hope she'd say yes.

I wait for a moment, then I sprint up the steps and toward the door, ready to open it and catch her before she leaves. But I can't open the door. I've never had a problem opening it before. I jerk it several times to see if it's locked. I keep trying until through the window I see an SUV driving away with a figure I assume is Marvel in the passenger seat. The man driving must be her uncle.

I keep yanking, and finally the door opens. Just like that.

I shut it and open the door again. Then try again, wanting it to get stuck to show me what happened. But it never does. The door opens fine every time I try.

Maybe some signs don't take a lot of figuring out. Maybe a sign like this happens and it's clear as day.

A closed door. Leave it closed.

But I yank the door open and head back into the store. I don't want this door to close, and I'm going to do everything I can to open it. Because I know—I know without a doubt—that's it's already opened just a crack.

It's just a tiny crack, but that's enough. That's not hypothetical. That's real. That's real and that's enough.

How are you?

I look at the late-night text and roll my eyes. For a while I just stare at it like it's a lost puppy looking at me through a glass window.

Fine. Busy trying to pay off my car. What's up?

I can't resist. I never could, to be honest. Until, of course, I'd had enough of Taryn's mind games and selfish, childish behavior.

I'm bored.

She's bored. That's why she's texting me. She's bored with summer already.

Must be nice to not have to worry about anything.

Be nice, she texts back. A few minutes later she adds, **Want to do something tomorrow?**

The timing of this is interesting. Part of me wants to say **Absolutely** and put Marvel's rejection behind me. But this is only because I'm angry about Marvel ending things before they started, not because I actually want to hang out with Taryn.

I can't.

Why not?

I don't want to be mean to her. **I'm busy.**

That's all I say. I wait to see if Taryn will push like she always does.

Okay. Good night.

It's left at that, which is good. The last thing I need now is Taryn. Any bit of Taryn. The school year ended, and so did Taryn and Brandon.

It's a new day, and Taryn is not a part of it.

I lie awake thinking about Taryn. I'm feeling guilty, which is crazy. I'm actually worried about Taryn Ellsworth, even though I know deep down she doesn't have feelings. Yet I still feel guilt because everything she said would happen actually sorta did. The only difference is she didn't mention the fact she'd turn out to be a nightmarish witch.

Taryn is the hot blonde every class seems to have. There's not an ounce of fat on her body and her skin never seems to sunburn and her hair never needs to be lightened because it's just that perfect. Her parents have a big place over in Glenforest Estates where a lot of the best high school parties are held. Taryn isn't a dumb blonde though. No, she's smart. A little *too* smart.

Sophomore year, I started chasing after her as if my life

depended on it. I'm a soccer player, not a football stud. My family isn't wealthy, and it's not like I'm *that* much of anything (good-looking, funny, athletic). But somehow I wore her down. I told her I loved her. I told her I'd do anything for her. And for a while, I really thought I did love her. For a while, I really did do anything.

Two things happened our junior year. The first was that we had sex. It wasn't the first time for Taryn, and I lied and told her it wasn't the first time for me. Somehow everything changed a bit after that. Not because suddenly I had no interest in her. It was more because of how normal Taryn acted afterward, as if it was the same as going out for ice cream. Nothing changed with her, and this made me a bit nervous. And confused.

The other thing was that Taryn became more and more mean. She was an upperclassman now, and she acted like it. She only hung out with juniors and seniors, or the occasional person of elite status in the lower grades. She made fun of others, many times with me at her side. I'd overlooked her snotty attitude because of my conquest. But suddenly I began to feel that this girl was cruel and vicious.

Then she went from being mean to also being racist. And it happened to be aimed at one of my guys.

All the football players were at a party after a big win. Taryn had too much to drink and started talking about Frankie being lucky to be on a team with so many great players. Frankie was the main reason the team was winning, but not according to Taryn. I actually began debating her about this, something I'd never done before. You just don't argue with Taryn in public unless you want to feel the brunt of her ridicule. Maybe it was because she was furious at me for talking back, or maybe because she was drunk, but she ended up using the N-word when talking about Frankie. Actually, she used it several times.

That was my wake-up call. Shortly after that, I broke up with her. At first she apologized and blamed a whole bunch of things for her rant: the alcohol, then a prescription she was on, then her mother, then other things. When that didn't work, she began to tell me that all I'd wanted was one thing, and when I got that I moved on. I told her she was a terrible person. It got more and more ugly. Then she finally decided to ignore me the rest of the year.

I think about all of it again and tell myself she's just not a nice person. That's putting it mildly. She's pretty much a terrible person who's been allowed to stay terrible because of her looks. I've often thought about this since, how we can't help what we're born with, whether it's an ability to throw a football or an attractive face or a set of rich parents. Or maybe it's none of those things, but instead it's a father who hits you. We can't help that. But we can help who we become.

It took you a long time before you wised up.

Maybe Taryn is a little right. Maybe I did get what I wanted and moved on. But I don't believe that. I think I finally was able to see who she was and didn't like it.

I think about Marvel and the conversation we had today. I wonder who she really is and why she doesn't want to get involved. A part of me knows I'm not going to pay any attention to this. Maybe I'll do what I did with Taryn. Maybe I'll just keep trying.

Maybe, hopefully, it'll end better than it did with Taryn.

16

A few days later, Devon sends me a link to an article about Artie Duncan's death. I just scan it because it's long and detailed, but several phrases stick out.

His body was found naked with his throat slashed from ear to ear and his chest stabbed over a dozen times.

Police have yet to identify a motive in the killing.

"It's an unspeakable tragedy. His parents are completely grief-stricken," says a neighbor.

This makes me feel a bit woozy. Hearing Artie got murdered is one thing. Hearing exactly how makes me feel kinda sick.

I think again about what Devon told me. It makes me wonder if the death did indeed have something to do with drugs. For someone to do a thing like this, maybe Artie was involved with something more than pot. Maybe things went bad. Like really, really bad.

When I get to Fascination Street I hear that Marvel called in sick. It also turns out that Harry is out for the day, and in his place is the all-things-cool-man Phil, the guy with the gray ponytail who seems to think it's still the seventies.

"So what did Marvel say?" I ask him.

"She's out. Can't make it."

Phil has never been one for long sentences.

"Did she say why?"

"She's sick, brother. That's all I need to know."

I wonder what Phil looks like behind his thick beard and sunglasses. I also wonder about his past and how he ended up here.

"Did she say what's wrong?"

"You don't ask a woman what's wrong. You never ask a woman what's wrong."

I laugh, but can't tell if he's making a joke or not. I'm thinking maybe he's not. Some old seventies tunes are playing, a little louder than normal. It's going to be a long day.

"Did you hear about Artie Duncan?" I ask Phil.

He nods and doesn't even look at me.

"What do you think happened?"

"I think the world is full of sickos. I think the world is different from when I was your age. I would think there's no hope. But I know there is."

I wait for more, but nothing comes. Phil has a cross tattooed on one forearm, five strange symbols on the other. Maybe the guy believes in God, though I'm thinking he only believes in the god of reefer and other happy drugs. Maybe his hope is in a big, fat joint he can smoke.

"Scary stuff," I say to him.

"Don't be scared. Be smart."

I manage to leave the record store before it's dark outside. I remember what Phil said, but I don't think "smartness" has anything to do with it. Was Artie stupid? Is that why he ended up getting his throat slashed? A car passes me, and the driver waves. I recognize him as a neighbor from down the street. His son is in my class. I wave back, but suddenly I feel a bit nervous. Who knows, he might be Artie's killer. Or maybe Phil did it. Or maybe it was Harry, or Devon's mother, or my father, or maybe it was Devon himself.

None of those make any sort of sense.

But I know the world doesn't make sense. It's nice to have teachers say *Here are the facts* and it's great to have preachers say *This is what you should believe*, but nothing really makes much sense these days. Facts and faith are really not that useful when you suddenly get nabbed from behind and taken somewhere and raped and killed. They didn't say Artie was raped, but I'm wondering why he didn't have clothes on.

Before I'm able to get coasting down the hill toward my house, I see a figure standing beside a brick building, watching me.

It's Marvel. And as I get closer to her, I see she's been crying.

17

"Are you okay?"

Marvel's standing in a doorway of the old brick building, but no cars are parked out front. I get off my bike and lean it against the building.

"No," she says.

"What happened?"

"It's just stuff at home," she says.

I know about stuff at home, I think.

I study her face, then her arms and anything else I can see. I'm looking for bruises.

"What's going on at home?"

She's wearing a Cubs hat and a sweatshirt with jeans. Nothing really matches, so it appears that she just grabbed something and dressed quickly before leaving the house.

"I was told I could trust you."

"By who?"

A car passes, and she leans back in the small doorway as though she's afraid to be seen.

She answers my question with another question. "You won't say anything to anybody, will you?"

I feel a strange dizziness, and I'm not sure why. It's the same feeling I've gotten around Marvel from the very beginning. It's not just being attracted to her. It's totally different from any sort of feeling I ever had for Taryn.

"No, I won't say anything," I assure her. "What do you need to tell me?"

Her look says enough. Those dark eyes and round cheeks seem so heavy, so weighted down.

"What is it?" I ask.

"It's my uncle. It's just—it's the way he looks at me."

I nod. "Has he . . . ?"

"No. He's never touched me. My aunt caught him snooping on me and they argued, but I feel like I'm the one who got in trouble. She acts like she doesn't trust me. I can feel the oppression in that house."

"Oppression? What do you mean?"

"Do you believe in demons, Brandon?"

I shrug. "Yeah, sure." I think of my father.

"I mean real, true demonic activity."

I think of the last horror movie I saw. "Yeah, I guess."

Marvel's eyes study me.

"What is it?" I ask, suddenly feeling like I said something wrong.

"I don't know what it is, why every single thing seems to be leading me this way."

"Every single what? Leading you where?"

"I was told to go to Fascination Records. I thought it was for some other reason. Now I believe it was to meet you."

The mystery—no, not just the mystery, but the vagueness of what she's saying—is a bit too much. So I make a joke. "You were destined to meet me," I say with a smile. "Maybe you were destined to be with me."

"Or maybe I was destined to save you."

"Save me? Save me from what?"

She shakes her head and sighs. "I don't know. I ask. Every day, Brandon, I ask God why. I ask him to show me. I ask him to reveal his will. And every time, he shows me the same thing."

"And what's that?"

"You."

18

Dad is waiting when I open the door to our house.

"Where's my money?"

"What money?"

I look around for my brothers, but they must be upstairs or in the basement.

"The money you owe me for your trashed car."

"I'm earning it back."

My father isn't that big, barely taller than I am, but he's all mean muscle. He's always worked out and still does. Which is why it really hurts when he moves across the room and slaps the back of my head.

"Empty your pockets," he says.

I show him that they're empty.

"Your wallet."

I slip it out and open it up. There's maybe ten bucks in there.

"What do you think you're doing?" Dad asks. He's drunk but not totally blasted. Something else is going on.

"I'm working every chance I get."

"So what are you spending it on? Huh? You think I'm an idiot? I know you're into something no good."

He hits me again, this time against the side of my head, almost knocking me off my feet. "Don't give me that smug look," he says.

"I'm not giving you any look."

He grits his teeth and stares at me, but there's something missing in his eyes. Something totally gone.

"You need to give me money every time you walk into this house, you got that? Every single time you use something that's *mine*. You understand?"

I'd love to talk back, to hit back, but I know better.

"Yes, sir," I say.

There's no sarcasm or irony or even a hint of rebellion in my voice.

I think back to my conversation with Marvel about how God told her to come into my life. That's nice, because maybe she can ask God to help me out a bit. In some small or big way. Maybe lightning can strike down Dad. Maybe a car can run him over. Or maybe the killer who did that to Artie could also do it to Dad.

I wouldn't care. I wouldn't care a bit.

When I go upstairs a moment later, I see the light on in my parents' bedroom. Mom works long hours and takes pills for sleep. Sometimes I think she takes too many, but I'd swallow a whole box of them if I had to sleep next to that monster. I wonder for the millionth time if she knows what Dad does to me. Alex and Carter have some idea. I tell them to just stay as far away from him as they can. As long as I can protect them from his craziness, I will. One day I'll stand up to him. One day I'll force things to go down. But for now I'll just continue to take it.

In my room, I lock the door and turn on my computer. Sometimes I wish I could not just friend people on Facebook, but also get magically transported to their world. Maybe I could end up in Devon's room or Frankie's apartment, or maybe I could find Marvel and somehow show up in her favorite place in the world. Anywhere but here. Anywhere but this house that will never feel like home.

I try to find Marvel again, but no luck. I should ask her if she has an e-mail address and whether or not she's on any social networks. I just want to connect. Even if I have nothing to say, I want to reach out and know she's there. To hear from her and crack a joke. To try to forget that I'm basically a prisoner in this house and that maybe she is a prisoner too. I want to hear a simple hello. But once again, I can't find her. It's like she's a ghost. Or maybe an angel.

There's a link from someone that shows a page that's supposed to be "Hilarious!" I click it and see a meme on a page someone from our high school has set up. I might have seen it before, because some of the pictures and quotes look familiar. But tonight I see a picture of someone I recognize. It's Seth Belcher, and he looks like he's either laughing or coughing by his locker. The caption says it all: *This is what happens when you read comics and take drugs.*

Nothing I've ever seen about Seth suggests he's taken drugs. I try to find out who posted the photo, but I can't.

I stay on Facebook for a while until I've had enough. I see some pictures of Taryn by a lake (wearing a tiny bikini). I see posts by Devon talking about Artie's death. Everybody has a different opinion, and they all share it. They share way too much. Some joke and some are freaked out. Oh, and there's another picture of Taryn wearing nothing and flaunting it.

I turn off my computer and wish I could do the same for my life. Just reboot it and suddenly find all the memory and viruses gone. Hear the "bong" sound on my MacBook and find that Dad and Mom and my brothers and my life are all running fast and smoothly without any problems or hitting or meanness. That would be pretty cool. But that's impossible.

As impossible as bringing Artie Duncan back to life again. Or finding Marvel online and talking to her.

19

On my way to work a few days later, I spot a couple of guys in a silver Camaro. They're wearing sunglasses and blasting their music, and at first I don't pay them any attention. Until I realize the driver is Greg Packard, the big football player I hit with a baseball bat.

We look at each other for a second. Then I start pedaling down the road as fast as I can.

It's lunchtime, but hardly anyone is around. I hear the squeal of tires and know that this race is going to be short and silly. I ride up onto the sidewalk so they won't run me over (at least not without jumping the curb). The car honks several times and I hear howling.

You're gonna get your face beat in.

Suddenly I'm the fastest cyclist in the world. I race down the sidewalk. I'm halfway down the street, the Camaro shadowing me on the road, when a garage door opens and a minivan begins backing up. I swerve back into the street and nearly hit Greg's car as I slam on my brakes, then start riding toward the sidewalk on the other side.

I have an idea.

The Camaro slows down, and I hear my name called out. The minivan drives off the other way, so any thought of help from the soccer mom is gone. Greg is hurling curses my way and shouting something about payback.

There's a small trail leading to the steps that head down to the quarry. I ride my bike all the way to the edge of them, then slip off the bike, pick it up, and start down the stairs. If I trip I'll be in trouble because the bike's weight will carry me down. But I make it all the way down before I hear some shouting above me.

"Brandon! You can't hide forever!"

Greg is standing at the top of the stairs. I suck in air and look at him. I know he's not going to bother heading down the hundreds of wooden steps. He'll just wait for another time.

"I'll find you!" he shouts.

I know he will. Who knows what will happen when he does.

I'm pedaling up a small incline on the road that leads back to town. As I do, I see a black Lincoln driving toward me at a pace similar to mine. The car looks new and freshly washed and polished. As it passes, I glance at the driver, who has his window down. An old, bald guy who looks as though he was born with a frown on his face looks at me with a *what-are-you-doing-around-here* expression, then rolls up his window and drives on.

I try to memorize the image. I wonder if this is Otis Sykes.

If it is, no wonder he lives alone by a quarry. He's like Shrek hiding his ugliness in the forest.

By the time I show up at Fascination Street I look like summer soccer practice has already started. Marvel gives me a funny look.

"Forget to take a bath?"

"I didn't realize my bike didn't have air conditioning," I say.

I'm not going to get into it about the guys following me. I want this girl to date me, not counsel me.

"What are you doing?" I ask, to change the subject.

"I'm organizing T-shirts."

"The excitement never stops. Can I help?"

"After you towel off."

I look at her and smile. Even though I won't earn a penny being here today, I'm glad to be here.

"So are you going to tell me no again?" I ask Marvel.

The store is closing and it's Friday evening. We've talked and laughed all day long, and there's no reason why that should stop.

"I don't think I heard a question anywhere," she tells me.

"Do you want to hang out? Especially since God keeps telling you that you should?"

I see a serious look on her face. "Don't mock. I only told you that because I can trust you."

"I'm not mocking you—I want to hang out with you."

"Six hours isn't enough?"

I shake my head. "Nope."

"Don't you have friends to hang out with?"

"I'd rather hang out with you."

She's wearing another bright, flowery top and white pants. She's a bit more dressed up than usual, making me think that *maybe* and *possibly* she did that with the thought of our going on a date.

"Have you seen the zombie movie with Brad Pitt?"

"No, and I don't plan to," Marvel says. "I have enough of those in my life already."

I laugh, then think about what she said. "What do you mean?"

"Nothing."

"Are you calling me a zombie?"

"Hardly."

She walks out of the store, and I follow. It's been clear all day, but for some reason there's a dark cloud right above us. It's one of those lone clouds that looks like an orphan.

"Are you being picked up?" I ask her.

She shakes her head. "I'm walking home."

"You live that close?"

"It'll be a long walk, but that's okay."

"I'd drive you home, but . . . well, you know."

Marvel only smiles.

"How about we get some Chinese food? It's right across the street."

"I don't know."

"Weren't you *just* talking about how good an egg roll would be?"

It's funny, because everything about her gives off the impression that she actually wants to hang out. She's dressed up and has no ride, and she really was just talking about wanting to eat Chinese.

"Just think of it as you're still working," I say. "If the thought of being around me is so awful."

She rolls her eyes. "Fine. Let's go. And I never said that being around you is so awful. You know what I said."

"Something about your being destined to be with me?"

"No, I didn't say that either."

I follow her, and as I cross the street I feel the sprinkle of raindrops coming down. Everywhere I look there are clear skies, but I'm getting rained on.

"Are you coming?" Marvel asks, already across the street.

"Do you see this?" I say, pointing upward.

"Someone's trying to get your attention."

"Yeah, but why?"

"You'll have to ask him."

I run toward Marvel, who is already walking down the sidewalk toward the Chinese restaurant. Maybe she really is just wanting an egg roll and doing me a favor. But I don't care. It's Friday night, and I finally have the date I've wanted the last couple of weeks.

20

I spend a bunch of time talking about Appleton High and about my family. By the time our meal comes, I wonder if Marvel is getting tired of me talking. "Sorry to keep rambling."

I realize I've actually been quite nervous for the last fifteen minutes.

"You know what I like about you?" she asks.

"There's something you like?"

"You never ask me about my family."

"So tell me about your family."

She shakes her head and takes a bite of her Szechuan chicken.

"The thing about this school year is that nobody here knows me. Nobody knows my family or my history or my story."

"Is that good or bad?"

"It's marvelous."

I laugh. "Was that a pun?"

"No. It's an adjective."

She takes another bite and smiles. I have a hard time knowing if she's teasing with me or not.

"So where do you see yourself after high school?"

"I don't," Marvel says.

"You don't what?"

"I don't see myself after high school."

"Don't you want to go to college?"

"I'd love to," she says. "But I don't think it's in the plans."

"Too expensive?"

For a minute she thinks about my question. "Yes. Yes, I think I can say that it's too expensive."

My sweet-and-sour pork doesn't interest me as much as this conversation. "Talking with you is always confusing."

"It's only confusing when you ask questions."

"Good point."

"I know how you can fix that."

I smile. "I'm just curious."

Marvel looks out the window next to our table. For a moment she seems deep in thought. "Want to know what I'm curious about?" she asks.

"Yeah."

When she looks back at me she still seems far away.

"I'm curious about what will happen when we take that last breath."

I didn't expect that. "That's kinda morbid."

"No it's not. Don't you wonder? I wonder, will

I suddenly be up there in the heavens? Will I see God's face the moment it happens, or will I have to wait? And if I do wait, will I be impatient, or will I be content to simply soak in everything?"

"I don't really like thinking about death."

Especially when guys in Camaros are chasing after me.

"It's not death I'm thinking about," Marvel says. "It's what happens next. I just wonder—I wonder what sort of memories I'll have. What kinds of thoughts and feelings I'll take with me. I think I'll remember everything, but I'll remember in a different way."

"Remember what?"

She looks back outside. "The awful stuff. The dark stuff. The stuff we don't want to think about but are forced to."

For a second I picture my father's face, then try to do everything possible not to think about him.

"Wouldn't it be nice?" she asks.

I nod. "Yeah, to blink and forget about all the crap."

"No, not to forget. But to make peace with it. Or more like to *have* peace about it."

"I spend my time thinking about how to get my car paid off."

Marvel nods. "I know. I think about what it's going to be like next year. I think about all that stuff. All the temporary things. But you know—what happens when you suddenly don't have time anymore? When the clock isn't ticking?"

"I just hope I'm not stuck fishing like my grandfather used to say. 'Cause if so, heaven's gonna be pretty boring."

She puts her fork on her half-eaten food. "It might be a lot of things, but boring isn't one of them."

"Singing choir songs could get old."

"Singing about being rescued will never get old. Never."

When we eventually get the bill, Marvel forces me to split it. I follow her outside and tell her I wish I had a car to drive her home.

"I'm happy to walk."

"Can I at least ride my bike along?"

It's just after eight, and the sun hasn't completely faded away, so it's not like it's totally dark.

"I'll be okay."

"You say that in a pretty confident way," I say.

"Because I mean it."

"Not to be dark, but you're the one talking about death."

"I'm talking about freedom," Marvel says.

"You know a kid our age was found in the river a couple of weeks ago?"

She nods.

"I want you to be safe."

"It was a male who was found," she says.

"That's comforting."

"I'm just saying."

We're standing on the sidewalk near Main Street that will take her over the river and back home. I'd love to kiss her, though I know this isn't the time or place. We're not even at the "I kinda like you" stage, at least as far as Marvel is concerned. I stare at her for a moment, not sure what to say.

"I can read your mind," she says.

I raise my eyebrows. "I don't think so."

She nods. "Boys. You're all the same."

"You're nothing like the girls at our school."

"I know."

"How do you know?"

"'Cause I know," Marvel says. "There's a reason I'm different. That's why I'm still here."

I'm confused. "Still here . . . you mean still hanging out with me?"

"Sure," she says in a way that makes it sound like I have no idea what she's talking about. "Good night, Brandon."

"Be careful, okay? I'd tell you to text me when you're home, but you don't have a cell phone."

"Says who?"

"You do?"

"I just don't like giving out my number," she says.

Then she walks away.

21

I'm sitting on the curb drinking an energy drink that Ms. Middleton gave me, feeling like I've mowed a dozen lawns. Ms. Middleton has a massive lawn, but I cut her grass for free. Her husband died a couple of years ago in a really bad car accident, so when she called one day and asked what I charge, I told her I'd do it for free. At least she gives me something to sip on afterward.

I don't notice the car slowing down and parking across the street until I hear a car door open and close and see a guy walking toward me. He's maybe in his thirties and looks like some kind of salesman.

"Are you Brandon Jeffrey?" he asks.

"Yeah."

For a second I wonder if I'm in trouble. Or if Dad has done something really, really bad.

"Can I ask you some questions about the death of Arthur Duncan?"

It's weird to hear Artie called Arthur. Is the guy a reporter?

"I'm Detective Passini," he says.

Don't they only talk to suspects?

I stand up and probably look way too nervous.

"Hot day to cut lawns, huh?" he says, offering his hand.

I shake it and smile, not knowing what to say.

"Were you good friends with Artie?"

"No. He was a year ahead of me."

"But you knew him, right?"

"Yeah, sure. Everybody knew Artie. Everybody liked him."

The guy nods in a casual, just-having-chitchat sort of way.

"What would you say about his friends? His close friends?"

"He had a lot of friends. He didn't have a close group, that I know of."

"Anything odd about his behavior this past year? Anything you can think of?"

For a second I try to remember anything that stood out. "He had a big part in the musical last year. Not that that's odd, but it's odd to someone who can't sing or act."

"Do you know anybody who had anything against Artie?"

I shake my head as I glance back at the freshly cut lawn. I wonder if Ms. Middleton is watching us, trying to figure out what's going on.

"He was seriously one of the most-liked guys at school."

Detective Passini nods, then studies me a bit. "You know, I've heard that about you, too."

"What? From who?"

"A variety of people."

I wonder if the variety is Devon, Frankie, and Barton.

And I wonder if he knows anything about Artie's little side job.

"I just wanted to give you a heads-up," he says. "To be careful."

"Do you guys know anything?"

"Here's my card. If you see anything strange—anything at all—you let me know. I'm giving my name to several students at the school just to try to have eyes and ears everywhere."

I think of the weirdo guy living in the woods near the quarry. But I don't say anything about him.

"Make sure you stay in groups, okay?"

His warning seems ominous.

"Do you think this might happen again?"

"We're doing everything we can to find whoever did this. So any help you might have—anything—let me know."

I say good-bye and watch him drive away. I glance at the house across the street with its blinds closed. Then I notice the one next to it with the fence around it. And the next house, which has a *For Sale* sign on it and looks abandoned.

A whole street full of people who could be killers for all I know. Who knows who is living beside you? We still don't really know the new neighbors who moved in next to us a year ago. It's too easy to go upstairs and play video games or go on the Internet and check Facebook. It's way too easy to ignore the obvious.

Maybe that's why what happened with Artie was way too easy. Maybe 'cause nobody else was paying him any attention.

Everybody's too busy in their own little worlds. Too busy until a dead body comes floating down the river and interrupts everyone's lives.

"Maybe there's a secret cult in Appleton," Barton says.

I look at his round face and shake my head. "You've watched too many horror movies."

"I was telling him that this town is a little odd," Devon says.

I'm doing my part and hanging out with the guys, since it's late at night. We've made a Sonic run and are sitting at a table outside eating ice cream. And watching Barton eat onion rings.

"Odd doesn't mean you have an evil cult hiding out somewhere," I say.

"If there is one I'm in trouble," Frankie says.

"Why?"

"'Cause," he answers, "the black dude is always killed off in horror movies. *Always.*"

This gets a big laugh from all of us.

"Nobody go swimming in any ponds or lakes," Barton says with his mouth full. "Instant death."

"Who goes swimming in lakes in the middle of the night anyway?" Devon asks.

"Hot girls who need to skinny-dip," Barton answers. "At least, in the movies."

"This isn't a movie," I say.

"Yeah, but someone did die," Barton says. "And died like in a really bad way."

I told them about the detective asking me questions. I didn't tell them what he said about my being a likable guy.

"You think someone just spotted Artie and decided, 'Yeah, I'm going to kill him'?" Frankie asks.

"I think there's something bigger going on here," Barton says.

"You're just trying to freak us out."

"No I'm not. What? Are you freaked out?"

"I'm going to dream of men in black robes," I joke.

"That's so cliché," Devon says. "Worst plot device you could think of, putting the weirdo townspeople in robes. Please."

"That would freak me out," Frankie says.

"You know what freaks *me* out?" Devon asks. "It's not knowing. It's thinking that the woman you've seen drive by a thousand times on your street might actually be storing someone in her basement."

"It's usually a plain, average white dude," Frankie says. "Like Brandon."

We laugh.

"The star quarterback is always the first to go," I joke back.

"So then I'm doubly gone."

It dawns on me that we're making cracks about death while a guy our age was brutally murdered. I want to say something, but I can't. Maybe we're joking because it helps us talk about all this.

"I heard Artie's mother is on suicide watch," Barton says.

"Where do you get this stuff?"

"I tell you, I know," he says.

"You're going to be one of those tell-all online reporter guys when you grow up," I say.

"The kind everybody hates," Frankie adds.

We're laughing when I spot the car. It's an old black Trans Am with wings on the hood. Its engine seems to shake everything around as it drives by.

That's the car that picks up Marvel.

The guy behind the wheel of the muscle car looks like trouble. Like Greg Packard trouble. No, actually worse than Greg Packard trouble. He looks like he thinks he's something special. He also looks mean.

One reason not *to try too hard with Marvel.*

The car rumbles by. I think maybe the opposite is the case: Maybe this guy is one reason I *should* be around Marvel. Because she's got that dude living with her and maybe she needs some help.

You let your own father beat up on you. What are you going to do for Marvel?

Devon and Frankie and Barton are still talking and laughing, and I join in. For now, I don't have to worry about anybody beating up on anybody unless it's one of us teasing the others.

I guess the detective was right. There is safety in numbers.

22

It's the last week in June, and I've made a decision. No more games. No more waiting around. No more maybes. Of course, I don't think Marvel has played games or waited on me or ever told me a maybe. *Nevertheless*, I plan on asking her out in an official capacity and showing up at the Teeds' annual July 4 bash with her at my side.

Every year, Devon's family has a big party where family, friends, neighbors, and sometimes, it seems, even strangers come to celebrate the Fourth. The Teeds live close to the park that hosts the fireworks, so everybody either stays and watches from their front lawn or walks a few blocks to see them up close.

I can't remember a Fourth of July I haven't hung out with Devon since I met him in sixth grade. Sometimes my brothers have come with me to hang out at his house. It helps that they have a pool.

Devon's parents are an interesting pair. His mother is

friendly and a talker, while his father is tall and thin like Devon and always seems busy. Mr. Teed doesn't say much— he's always fixing something or cooking something or doing something. Which is far better than my father, who never does any of those things unless he's trying to fix the face of his eldest son.

With July 4 five days away, I'm both looking forward to it and dreading it. Some of the worst things in my life have happened around holidays. For some reason holidays make people like my father even more crazy than usual. Maybe it's the heat and the fireworks and the fact that everybody is at home trying to celebrate something.

Harry's having a big weeklong sale, so the record store has been busier than usual. Lots of people wanted me to cut their lawns before the holiday, so my week has been crazy busy. But so far, no teenager has gone missing from home, and I haven't gotten punched in the back of the head. So life is good. And since it's good, I'm going to make it better by asking Marvel out.

The album being cranked (and it's really loud even for the store) is by a band called INXS. It's called *Shabooh Shoobah*, and that got Marvel and me joking for an hour. Today she's wearing a bandanna thing that matches her dress, and wooden-like platform shoes that make her as tall as me. If I didn't know her I would've laughed, but now her outfits are something I wait to see. Harry and I always have to comment on them.

I'm waiting for the right moment, maybe right after we

both get off work, or maybe sometime when Harry slips out. I'm trying to think of the right words to say to her.

I know we sorta went out, but I want to go on a real date with you.

Something like that.

I know that you don't want to get involved, and I respect that, but I'm hoping I can change your mind.

Not something like that. That's lame.

Look, I'm not trying to . . .

"Brandon?"

I turn around and see Marvel standing in the aisle. I don't see Harry or anybody else.

"I'm meant to be with you, okay?"

For a second, as the drums and the guitars and the singer all wail away, I stand there and stare at her as if she just spoke in a foreign language.

"No tengo ni idea de lo que acabas de decir."

Yep, I have no idea.

"So look, it's fine just as long as you know that there can't be anything between us, not like *that*. You know?"

Uh, what?

"Okay," I say.

"I know, I know, that makes no sense. I'm not making any sense."

"No, you're not."

"But listen—this is what I have to do. What? What is it?"

"What?" I ask.

"Why do you have that look on your face?"

"What look?"

"That . . . that know-it-all smirk."

I laugh. I don't know it all. I don't know anything, in fact. "Do you have plans for the Fourth?" I ask.

"I guess I do now," Marvel says.

She says it the way I might say I need to mow Ms. Middleton's lawn. So strange. So very strange. But I'm not going to complain. I'm not going to question her either.

"My buddy's family has a big party before the fireworks, and I always go."

"Then I'll be going too."

Harry comes back in and heads to the counter. Marvel takes that as a cue that our conversation is over.

That was the easiest asking-a-girl-out ever.

23

Horror movies don't scare me. It's the weekend before July 4, and I go with the guys to see a new scary movie that's getting a lot of buzz. It's gross and has a bunch of moments when the audience groans in disgust or everybody laughs because it's crazy bizarre. But I never get spooked or feel a bit of anxiety watching it.

Afterward we all pile into Devon's Jeep, wondering what to do next on this Saturday night.

"That part with the father killing his son—now that's sick," Barton says.

"Could an ax actually do that?" Devon asks.

"I wouldn't want to find out."

"I mean—you'd have to hit it just right to decapitate someone with one swing," Devon continues.

"Not 'someone.' His own son."

"That was ridiculous," I say. "The head went flying like a basketball."

"And his girlfriend catches it," Barton howls from the backseat.

"I think the new wave of terror is going to be movies where they don't show anything," I say. "Not even blood."

"It's like playing a video game," Frankie says. "You see a head spinning and it's like, 'Okay, whatever.'"

"What if that really happened?" Barton says.

"Then you'd be dead."

"No, I mean, could you imagine seeing a real human head spinning by you?"

It's a pretty ludicrous conversation, but then again the movie we just saw was pretty ludicrous. Barton makes us laugh describing what people would say if they caught a human head that's just been decapitated.

"You were a lot prettier stuck on a body."

We all howl.

"It's so nice to snuggle with you."

"Sick," Frankie says.

"What am I supposed to do with *this*?" Barton says in some old person's voice.

"Mrs. Gabhart!" That's the hundred-year-old librarian at our high school.

We're passing close to Maxwell Park, which is right across from the school. We're still laughing when we feel the car hit something and then drive over something metallic. Barton curses, and Devon slows down.

"What was that?" he asks me.

My window is open and I look out into the darkness. I see something on the side of the road that shines from the reflection of the taillights.

"It's a bike," I say.

"I drove over a bike?"

"Was there someone on it?" Barton asks.

"I don't see anybody."

Devon stops the Jeep and waits as I get out and check out the bike. The one tire looks flattened like a pancake. I look toward the side of the road where a small street heads toward Maxwell Park. In another few days this place will be mobbed with people as they pick out places to sit to watch the nearby fireworks.

"Anybody around?" Devon asks.

I tell him no and try to prop up the bike, but it won't stand.

"Did my car get damaged?"

I go to the front and examine the bumper, then check out the tire. I hear crickets in the background along with Barton's voice in the car. I'm starting to sweat from the humidity.

"Hhhhhhhhheeeeeeeeeeee."

I jerk around and stare into the darkness. That voice didn't come from the Jeep but from out there, out where I can't see anything.

"Hey guys, help me," the voice calls.

For a second I wonder if a head is going to go hurling past me. I can feel goose bumps covering my skin. I'm about to get back in the vehicle when a figure pops out of nowhere and starts walking down the street into the glare of the headlights. The figure is bony and white and naked. In his hands is a tattered shirt that he holds over his privates.

"I need some help."

As the figure gets closer, I recognize Seth. His nose is bloody and his eyes look swollen from crying.

"What happened?" I ask as I walk his way.

The guys in the Jeep are quiet now. I hear them getting out to see what's happening.

"Is that your bike?" Devon asks. "I think I might have hit it."

I don't think it dawns on Devon that he's talking to a kid who's not wearing any clothes and looks like he was just beat up. When I actually notice the white-as-chalk skin, I see there's writing on it. Lots of words I'd get in trouble for saying, and I live in a house where Dad curses all the time.

"Aw man, who did this?" Frankie asks.

"You're naked," Barton says.

"Here," I say as I take off my polo shirt and give it to him. "Devon, you got anything in your car?"

"Sweatpants are in the back in the bag," he says. "They need to be washed."

"Can you get them?"

"Who did this?" Frankie asks again.

"Football guys," Seth mumbles.

"Like who?"

"I know who," I say.

"Four or five of them."

"Same guys as before?" I ask.

"I don't know—maybe. I couldn't see. I was riding my bike and fell off when they ran me off the road."

"Those guys are screwed," I tell Frankie.

"You don't know who did it," he says.

"Oh, I know. The same morons who slashed the tires of my bike."

Seth is breathing heavily, hoarsely. Devon gives him the sweatpants, and he puts them on.

"They were drunk," he says in a whimper.

"Of course they were," I say.

"So they stole your clothes?" Barton asks.

"They were coming from a party."

"And they just spotted you riding your bike?" Frankie asks.

"I was meeting someone here," Seth says, still out of breath, his eyes barely staying open. "I was totally set up."

"Meeting them for what?" Barton asks.

I tell him to shut up.

"Are you okay? Did they hurt you anywhere?"

Seth shakes his head.

"Seriously, I know who did this," I tell Frankie.

"Why are you making it sound like I'm part of it?"

"'Cause you play on the football team."

"With a lot of good guys."

"And a few jerks," I say.

"I just want to go home," Seth says.

"I say you go to the cops and make a statement," I tell him, looking at the bloody T-shirt he was wearing before it got torn off of him. "Where're the rest of your clothes?"

"They took them."

Something about this makes me furious. "Let's go find those guys."

"We're not 'finding those guys,'" Frankie tells me. "Use your head."

Barton curses as he gets close to Seth and checks out his face. Frankie tries to fit the bike in the back, but it's too big.

"Leave my bike here," Seth says. "I just want to go home."

"Look, this is gonna keep happening," I tell him. "You gotta do something."

He gives me a detached and scary look, then shakes his head. "Please take me home."

I nod, then look at Devon. We all pile into the Jeep with Seth sitting up front. He guides Devon to a dead-end street I've never been down, toward some run-down homes.

"You live here?" Barton asks.

Sometimes I want to tell Barton to just shut up.

"Thanks," Seth says in a weak voice. Then he turns toward me. "Again."

"This isn't going to happen again," I tell him as I get out and try to shake his hand, then settle for patting him on the shoulder. "I swear it won't."

"Just let me know how I can give you back your shirt," Seth says.

He's a tall guy, taller than I am. He looks so pitiful.

"Yeah, sure, no rush. You know Fascination Records, close to downtown? The small record store on the corner? That's where I work."

"Okay."

We see his toothpick-like figure head toward the only home with a light on. I feel something inside I can't identify. It's not just anger. It's more than that. A lot more than that.

"There's nothing you can do," Devon tells me while he's driving us back to his house.

"The football team better start looking for someone to replace your boy Greg," I snap at Frankie.

"He's not 'my boy.'" Frankie is as frustrated as I am.

"He keeps you from getting sacked," Barton says.

"He's got issues," Frankie says.

"Yeah, and he's got more tonight," I mutter.

"I don't know if I'd get involved," Barton says.

"We *are* involved," I say. "*We.*"

"No way," Barton says. "I'm not going to get stripped down on the side of the road by the football players."

"That would be an unfortunate sight," Devon says, and we all laugh.

"An 'unfortunate sight'!" Barton howls.

I laugh with them, but none of this is funny. A decapitated head being tossed around in a cheesy horror movie is funny, but seeing a poor kid like Seth naked on the street and unable to talk isn't funny. It's beyond not funny.

For a while I don't say anything as the car moves through the darkness.

"Greg is trouble," Frankie says. "I'm just telling you."

"I didn't even know this guy Seth before I saw him getting kicked all over the park that day."

"Greg's *father* is trouble," Frankie adds.

"He's a cop."

"Yeah."

He says this in a way that says he knows more, but that's all he says. It doesn't matter if Greg and his father are trouble—somebody needs to stop this. Some adult needs to know what's happening to Seth.

When we get to Devon's house, Frankie pulls me aside and tells me one last thing as the two other guys are heading into the house.

"Greg's dad, Sergeant Packard—he's going to make sure his son doesn't get kicked off the team."

"How do you know?"

"I know."

"What? How? Come on."

Frankie blocks my way into Devon's house.

"I know because I tried to get Greg kicked off at the end of last year," Frankie tells me. "Not only did it not work, but his dad threatened me."

"Shut up."

"I'm serious."

"Threatened you how?"

Frankie looks at the front door, then back at me. "He said he'd break both my arms if I said anything."

Marvel called in sick again today, but that's okay because she has a backup. A permanent backup working solely for the sake of being around her.

"Can I get paid for today?" I ask Harry.

"Well yeah, sure, since you're actually going to *work*."

His hair looks curlier than usual; the humidity outside is making it poof up like a popcorn kernel in the microwave.

"I work. What are you talking about?"

"You follow Marvel around like a puppy all day long."

"While I work."

"So is your big plan working?" Harry asks as he unrolls a poster he's going to frame and hang on the wall.

"There's no big plan."

"Is she into you?"

"Yeah, I think. Sort of. Maybe."

Harry looks over at me and shakes his head, laughing. "You'll learn one day."

"Learn what?"

"You can't win. They *are* the superior race."

"Who says I'm trying to win?" I ask.

"You're trying to control the situation. But I'm telling you, it won't work. Why do you think it was Eve who gave Adam the apple? He was just a dumb male like the rest of us."

I think about his statement for a minute. "You sound like you got in an argument at home."

Harry nods. "Oh, yeah, totally."

"Did you win?"

"Are you kiddin'? When a woman gives birth to your three children, she *always* wins. Come on, help me keep this poster flat for a second."

The minute I see the Hawaiian shirt and white legs in cargos and flip-flops, I know who's stopping by. Lee. I've been hoping that old guy would come in one of these days. I want him to meet Marvel. Unfortunately, she isn't here.

"Got any good Beach Boys records?" he asks me.

"None you don't already have."

Lee Fleisher is the town clown. He doesn't actually wear the makeup and costume, but he still sorta resembles one. He's nearly bald, and the hair on each side of his head is usually windblown, giving him a bad comb-over look. He was a businessman in Appleton until he retired years ago, but he still does motivational talks. I can't imagine Lee giving businesspeople motivational talks, but he's a millionaire with a lot of experience. Plus, he tells funny stories.

"What's up, Lee?" Harry says from behind the counter.

"Absolutely nothing." Lee wanders down an aisle at his usual pace.

He's an avid music collector and one of the reasons Harry stays in business. He's always buying albums and having us order stuff for him. He says his wife loves for him to play records and dance with her. Apparently she has something like Alzheimer's and doesn't ever come out of their large house in Glenforest Estates.

"That Vangelis record still hasn't come in," Harry tells him.

"I told you, I think it's out of print."

"They keep telling me it's in stock."

"Never trust people trying to make money off artists," Lee says. "You hear that, Brandon?"

"Yep."

"Tell me—what do you want to do when you grow up?"

"I want to be like you."

"What? Old, fat, and bald?"

I laugh. Lee is always making fun of himself, which is probably why he feels he can make fun of everybody else, too.

"I want to own a whole selection of Hawaiian shirts like you have."

"When I die I'll bestow them all to you. God knows our boys hate these things."

Lee is funny, especially when talking to ladies in the store. One day Harry's wife came in, and Lee wasn't even subtle about flirting with her. Harry couldn't believe how crude the old guy was, but she just laughed.

"Phil's not in, is he?" Lee asks.

"Not today," I say.

"That guy hates me."

I somehow can't see hippie Phil hating anybody. "Why would he hate you?"

"I just get that hate vibe from him."

"It's probably because you don't like seventies music," Harry says.

"I don't dislike it. I just don't get into the heavier stuff, the stuff you need drugs to like. Pink Floyd and all that."

"I bet you're not a fan of Dennis Shore then, huh?" Harry asks.

Dennis is a best-selling novelist living in Geneva. He stopped writing for a while after working hard to take one of his books out of circulation. Rumor had it that he'd plagiarized part of it or something like that. He's since started publishing again and even did a book signing at Fascination Street earlier this spring.

"That guy? What a hack. I can write better books than him."

"Big Pink Floyd fan."

"That explains a lot," Lee says. "I bet he only has half his brain cells left."

After a few minutes of waddling around like some big duck, Lee calls out to me. "Hey, Brandon. When are you going to come over and cut my grass?"

"I told you your lawn is too big."

"Bring help then. I'm just trying to support the local talent."

"Talent?" Harry asks.

"I bet this guy barely pays you," Lee says.

"If you only knew," I say.

"Come on. I love young entrepreneurs. I used to be one myself."

"What?" Harry asks. "Back in the twenties?"

"Yep," Lee says. "During the Depression. Tough times."

Lee loves to joke. But the thing is, this guy is loaded. I make a mental note to get someone like Frankie to help me cut his lawn. We might make some nice money, which is something I definitely could use these days.

I think of Marvel again and contemplate calling her at home. But I decide not to. Last thing I want to look like is a stalker. Or someone trying too hard.

I want to try just enough to have her suddenly figure out why she needs to be with me.

The guys and I are going swimming. On my way to the quarry I pass an old church building that's been empty for a while. I glance at it as I'm coasting down the hill toward the bridge to go over the Fox River, and I spot Marvel. She's heading into the church.

I call out, but the door shuts and she's already inside. I slow my bike down and prop it on the sidewalk. I see the date on the side of the church telling when it was built: 1846. I wonder when people stopped going to this big Baptist church. Ever since I can remember, it's been empty. I guess maybe if families like mine actually attended church on Sunday mornings, places like this would still be open.

For a while Mom tried to get us to go to church, but she eventually gave up. None of us really wanted to go. And once Dad lost his job and the financial pressure went onto Mom, having a "day of rest" meant sleeping in and not worrying about being somewhere at ten thirty.

I'm thinking maybe Marvel just walked into the building to check it out, so I wait outside for about five minutes. It's a clear, hot day, with cotton-ball clouds shuffling around in the sky. After I start to sweat, I decide to go inside and see what Marvel is doing.

The church looks as if it's been waiting for a congregation to come back and sit in its long pews for the last decade. It smells musty, and it's dark with grainy light coming in. Plus it's about as hot as the outside, except this is a thick heat like a blanket smothering you.

I see Marvel sitting in the middle set of three sections of pews. She's bent over, so I assume she's praying. I stand back and watch her, feeling like a weird stalker, feeling like I'm invading a very private moment.

Maybe tell her you're here before freaking her out when she sees you.

I almost cough as I enter the large sanctuary. The ceiling seems to tower ten stories above me. The cross on the back wall is lit up with reds and oranges from the reflection of the sun, almost sizzling. This place doesn't feel like a church. It doesn't feel holy. It only feels stuffy and empty.

I hear a whimper, and suddenly I realize Marvel is crying. I keep moving down one of the two aisles cutting through the church. Then I clear my throat.

"Marvel?"

Her head jerks back for a moment, and I see those dark eyes and round cheeks. She closes her eyes as if she's disappointed. I slide into the pew behind her and hear the cracking of the old wood as I sit down.

"What's wrong?" I ask.

"What are you doing here?"

Her voice is barely a whisper. It sounds weak, her nose stopped-up.

"I saw you on the street. I just—I called your name but you didn't hear me."

"So you followed me in here?"

"Why are you crying?"

She looks up at me, her face angry one moment, then suddenly sad again. She seems too tired to put up a fight. "It's just, sometimes it's all—" The rest of her words come out mumbled and incoherent.

I place an arm around her because I don't know what else to do.

"It's going to be okay," I say because I can't think of anything else to say.

"I know it will. That's what I'm trusting. That's what I tell myself every single day and every single night. I smile and know that God has given me this day for a reason, but still, sometimes . . . sometimes . . ."

She begins to cry.

"What?" I ask her.

"No, not—I don't mean to be like this. I'm not like this. Not like this. Like *this*."

"It's okay," I tell her, thinking whatever it is is something she'll get through.

"I moved here because my father murdered my mother and my sister and then killed himself."

I hold in a breath, unable to talk, unable to move.

It's not okay. It's definitely not okay and it won't ever be okay.

"God spared me for a reason, and I know that and I'm

thankful, but I still miss my family. I miss my sister. I miss the life I once had."

I still don't know what to say.

"Marvel—"

"There's nothing to say. It's okay."

She takes my hand as if she knows what I'm thinking.

Murdered? By your father?

"It was in the news," she says. "But my name was never mentioned. And people don't pay attention to the news, right? Someone gets killed in Chicago and nobody really notices. A crazy man decides to torch his family, but because they're Hispanic nobody really notices *that* much, right?"

"I'm sorry. . . ."

"I know," she says. "I am too. I'm sorry every single day, Brandon."

"But what happened? Why?"

She wipes her cheeks.

"Because there was a devil living inside of my father and it finally had had enough with my mother and her faith and her love of Jesus."

I want to ask a dozen questions, but they all seem so wrong and so unmentionable. I remain quiet, thinking of the weight this girl must be walking around with.

But most of the time she's so bright and happy.

"I knew I'd eventually tell you because these things get out. I just didn't know how. You've been so kind to me."

"Not really," I say.

"Yes you have. And I just—I'm just trying to figure things out."

"Like what?"

"Lots of things. The first one being you."

"What about me?"

She waits for a moment to talk, then looks back up toward the cross. "Brandon, do you believe there really was a man called Jesus Christ?"

I shrug. "Yeah, sure."

"No, really. Tell me the truth. Do you believe he was the Son of God and came down to be a real man and die on a real cross?"

"Umm—well . . ."

It's never been asked of me what I really and truly believe. I've accepted it the same way I accept that we need Christmas and Easter holidays.

"I've never seen the cross in the same way I see it now. Christ's death. For me. His saving *me*. I just—I'm so over-whelmed. Yet I still have days when I just feel beaten down."

"I'm sorry," I tell her.

"You didn't do anything. You've been there for me since I got here. Making me laugh and making me forget. Two very good things."

"I didn't know about your parents."

"How could you? I still don't understand the *why*, Brandon. I understand why God came down to this world to save us. It's because we needed to be saved. But why I was saved from the thing my father did . . . I will never know."

I want to ask details, but I also want to get out of here.

"Do you want to be alone?" I ask.

She laughs. "What do you think?"

"Um, yes?"

Marvel shakes her head. "Come on—let's go back outside."

26

Ten minutes later we're sitting across from each other at a deli eating sandwiches. One minute she's talking about her father who burned her whole family, next she's talking about how much she doesn't like pickles.

"Are you okay?" I ask.

"Of course."

She seems again like the Marvel I know. Confident, smiling, curious.

"I didn't know," I say again. I feel like I did something wrong in not knowing.

"I've been carrying this around ever since I came into the record store."

"I know—it's just . . ."

"God gives me daily strength. Some days—*most* days—I feel it walking with me. But some days I forget to bring it with. Like today."

She doesn't sound like a preacher at a church or one of

those Christian speakers trying to sell a product or something. She's sounding like this strength is something that is real, like a backpack she carries around with her every day.

"I love the verse in the Bible where it says God will wipe every tear from our eyes and there'll be no more death or sorrow or suffering, that they'll be gone forever. I know that's what heaven will be like. A place where nobody is sitting in a dark church crying. There won't be abandoned churches, for one. There won't be death or crying or pain."

I'm not very hungry, but I'm eating my sandwich to avoid talking. I swallow and nod at her comment. "That's a cool thought."

"I think about heaven a lot. Maybe people we always wondered about will one day pass by our open door. I like thinking that doors won't be locked there. Maybe the houses won't even have doors at all. It'll be like those hotels without doors I've seen pictured in exotic locations, inviting guests to enter and exit whenever they want. I like to think we will be pleasantly surprised by some of the guests who visit us. I think heaven is like a great surprise we'll experience daily, hourly. Goose bumps greeting us all the time. Never getting old. Never getting routine."

"You must think about it a lot," I say.

"This place is just a trailer for a film, Brandon. Our lives here. Heaven is like the movie. Except there's only one trailer before the movie. And the movie won't ever end."

"What if you need to get up and go to the bathroom?"

She laughs, which is good, because I don't know how much longer I can take this whole death-and-heaven conversation. It's not that I don't believe in it. I just don't have anything to add. Heaven sounds like a nice concept but also sounds very, very boring.

Unless Marvel is there and I could show up by her doorstep.

Good thing for me is that maybe I won't have to knock.

"Another verse I love is Psalm 32:7. 'For you are my hiding place; you protect me from trouble. You surround me with songs of victory.' I love the idea of being surrounded by songs."

"We're surrounded by songs every day," I say. "Unfortunately, many of them are eighties tunes."

Marvel laughs. "You can be funny, you know that?"

"It's usually when I don't have anything else to say."

"I know."

"You can be confident," I say. "You know that?"

"It's only because I pray daily and hourly for strength. I mean—I'm not trying to sound so spiritual or anything. But it's true."

I nod. She smiles, staring at me, then glances around as if to see if anybody is close to our table. We're on our own.

"When something like that happens—what happened with my family—there are only two directions you can go. You can head downward. Or you can cling to these morsels of truth. The words that have come long, long before you. You can choose to believe them. And that's what I do."

For a brief moment I think of doing something crazy, something I've never done before and vowed I never would. I almost tell Marvel the truth about my father. But I literally bite my lip to make it stay shut.

"It's hard sometimes," she says. "Many times. Like this morning."

"Sorry."

"But then I remind myself of God's unfailing love. Each morning that's what I do. I pray and ask him to bring me peace. And once again, he brings me the same thing."

"What's that?" I ask.

"You."

27

Later that night, after I've hung around with the guys but not said a word about Marvel's admission, I go online to find details of what happened. It takes me a while, but eventually I find an article that mentions Marvel in the comment box after it.

CHICAGO — A 38-year-old man burned down his home in Humboldt Park on Tuesday night. He was armed with an AK-47 rifle, apparently upset about family issues. Police say he prevented his wife and two daughters from fleeing the flames while keeping firefighters away. Miraculously, the older daughter managed to escape while the rest of the family, including the father, died.

Shots were reported, but police and firefighters did not arrive until the house was ablaze. Nobody else was injured in the fire.

Alonso Garcia had a history of domestic abuse issues and had been reported as acting erratic in the final days of his life.

The surviving daughter is now in the custody of her aunt and uncle.

The report is so simple, so impersonal, so lifeless. I still can't believe it has to do with Marvel. That she was the miracle described.

I hear the beep of a notification on my Facebook page. When I check, I see a friend request from Marvel Garcia.

So you do have a Facebook page.

After I accept her, I see a message box show up.

Thanks for today, she writes.

Thanks for adding me as a friend, I write back.

No problem.

How are you doing now? I type.

I hope you're not going to ask me that every time you see me now. There's a reason I don't tell people about what happened to me. I don't want them feeling sorry for me.

Just checking.

I'm doing well enough to befriend you on Facebook.

Well, that's something.

I was listening to a bunch of contemp. Christian songs. Feeling sorta melancholy tonight.

For a second I hesitate. What I'm thinking is, *Maybe you're feeling that way because your family was burned to a crisp by your father. I'd feel that way too.*

Instead, I ask who she's listening to. She lists some people I haven't heard of. I've heard of more of the stuff Harry plays in the record store than of the groups and artists she's talking about.

You know something I've always dreamt about? To hear my story told in songs. Songs about victory. Like that psalm I mentioned to you. I like to think that this all ends in a victorious way.

I wonder what she's talking about. **That what ends?**

Marvel doesn't respond.

I could see Justin Timberlake singing songs about me, I write back.

Definitely. Would you dance to those too?

Of course. I love to dance.

Me too, Marvel writes. **Maybe one day we can dance together.**

I don't know—lots of girls lining up to do that.

Then I'll just have to wait. I can do that.

Maybe I'll let you cut in line, I write to her.

What a gentleman. I kinda like you.

For a moment, I wonder what to say. It's a harmless thing, yet it still says so much.

Don't be afraid, she types. **It's just—you know something nobody else around here knows. So like it or not, you're stuck with me.**

I smile. **Sounds good to me.**

This is beyond understatement.

28

"Do you like this album?"

This is one of those weird days when Marvel isn't here. One of those days Harry will actually pay me for.

The album he's playing is weird. Dark and odd and quirky, the kind I'm not sure what to think of.

"It's the Cure," Harry continues.

"Okay." I'm thinking he's telling me just so I know.

"Come on—I've told you about them. They're the ones I got the name of the store from," Harry says.

Fascination Street. I remember him playing me the song not long after I started working here.

"So, you like these guys?"

"Sure." I say that as more of a *Sure?*

Harry laughs. "Hey, listen. I know you've been working hard even though you're stricken with Marvel."

"Stricken?"

"Yes. Stricken."

"That sounds like I'm sick or something," I say.

"You're working for free."

"Well, yeah. Except for days like today, right?"

Harry nods. "Look, I have something to give you. If you want it."

"What's that?"

"I got two tickets for Sunday at Lollapalooza."

I know Lolla well. It's a music festival for about a hundred groups and a hundred thousand people, all heading to Grant Park in Chicago. I've never been, but I've sure heard about it.

"You don't want to go?" I ask.

Harry laughs. "I've been the last few years. But I'm getting old, and I've been to a lot of shows already this summer. My wife sure doesn't want to go. I figured you might want to check it out. The Cure is the headliner."

The wailing voice and weird music I'm hearing don't really inspire me to rush over to Harry and grab the tickets.

"Trust me, they're good," Harry says.

"Okay."

"You want the tickets?"

"You think Marvel would go with me?" I ask Harry.

"You tell me. But yeah, I was thinking something like that."

"I don't know."

Harry looks up at me and rubs his beard. "Which? You don't know if you want to go, or you don't know if Marvel would go with you?"

"Both?"

"She knows you're slightly infatuated with her. You know that, don't you?"

"Yes?"

Harry laughs at my quasi-question response.

"I saw the Cure with my wife back in the early nineties. When I was your age."

"I'm not sure I'm going to marry Marvel," I say, kind of joking.

"Yeah, well, I didn't know I was going to marry Sarah. You never know, do you? Listen, I'd love to go, but there's a youth group retreat I gotta go to. So I figured I'd help you out."

"How's that?" I ask.

"Surprise Marvel. I think she'd go with you. Not because it necessarily makes sense, the two of you being together, but because there are always exceptions."

He hands me the two tickets, and I slip them into my pocket.

"Thank you."

But I'm not sure if I should really thank him. I'm not sure what to say.

"This will help," he says.

"How do you know I need help?"

He laughs. Like really super loud. "Guys like us always need help, Brandon. Remember that. Girls like Marvel, they're walking miracles. Guys like us, we're just road signs, hoping to catch their attention."

I'm not sure I like being considered a road sign.

"Look, I know. I get it. It's just—you gotta realize who you are. You gotta realize that sooner or later you might have to fight to win her over."

Harry disappears, and I wonder how he knows what's

going on with Marvel. But I hold the ticket and plan on asking her. Whenever I see her next.

Maybe I'll tell her Harry wants her to go.

Maybe I'll say her job depends on it.

Mom and I are in the old minivan we had hoped to get rid of a few years ago. It's a white Chrysler Town & Country, but it looks more like a rusted minivan that's been left out in the country a little too long. It makes strange squeaking sounds while you're driving, not to mention the brakes that start to wail at the worst moments.

Mom picked me up from work, and we're getting fast food before heading home.

"Are you glued to that like the rest of the world?" Mom asks after I've been on my iPhone for five minutes.

Mom is no-nonsense about a lot of things. Because she never has extra time, she tends to be impatient and short with words. She doesn't mean to be gruff; it's more because she doesn't have time to talk about nothing like so many other grown-ups I know.

"I stay off this at work."

"You like the record store?"

I nod.

"What about the pretty girl who works there?"

Mom saw Marvel when she came in to let me know she was parked outside.

"She's cool."

Mom looks straight ahead and gives me a *yeah right* laugh. "She seems interested in you."

"Oh, yeah, totally," I say in complete mockery.

"Trust me. Women know."

"You say that to us all the time," I reply.

"It's because we know."

I don't answer, but I think about Dad. Mom may know a lot, but she doesn't know everything.

"What's her name?"

"Marvel. Short for Marvella."

"You should invite her over for dinner sometime."

"I think I'd rather get run over by a tractor."

"It can't be that bad."

"Trust me," I say. "It'd be bad. She's not ready for that. I'm not ready for it either."

"She seems really nice."

"She is."

Our car whines its way through the drive-through line at Arby's. Mom laughs at the sound it's making. "One of these days this is simply gonna give up the ghost," she says, more to herself than to me.

"So we have a haunted minivan? Awesome."

Mom taps my head as if I'm still ten. "You can be so witty at times."

"I try."

"I don't think I'll always be this busy," she says as we wait for our food. She ordered enough for a football team. "I think this summer is just extra stressful."

"It's fine. We're all fine."

"Yeah," she says. "Well, most of you anyway."

Now's your chance, tell her, tell her now before the guy asks if you want horsey sauce, do it.

But I can't. I don't say another word. That moment, the moment that never comes around, was suddenly right there in front of me. But I can't. I can't do this to Mom.

I'm fine.

So I tell myself. So I tell her and the rest of the world.

30

Later that night, I'm walking out of the theater with Frankie when I see a group gathering around a car. I see that it's a Camaro.

"Don't go over there," Frankie says.

I hear laughter and then someone yelling. "What's going on?"

"You don't want to know."

But somehow I think I already know. I think this has happened once before.

"Brandon, come on," Frankie says, trying to pull me toward his car.

But it's not happening. I move toward the group of six guys standing there laughing and calling out. When I get to the circle, I see Greg, fists clenched, towering over someone. The guy on the ground is on his hands and knees, struggling to stand. It looks like they've started a fight club right outside the Appleton Cinema 16.

I'm not surprised to see it's Seth Belcher on the ground.
His face is bloody. He coughs.

"Get back up," Greg yells at him.

I move into the circle and grab Seth. He's so bony, so light.
I pull him up.

Greg curses. "Brandon, what are you doing?"

Now someone is by my side. Frankie.

"Davis, man, what are you doing?" Greg asks his
quarterback.

"Saving his life."

"Whose?"

"Both," Frankie says. "What are you doing?"

"We're having a little fun."

I notice Greg is wearing Seth's kamikaze bandanna around
one of his fists. It's splattered with blood. Seth is unsteady on
his feet, so I help him stand still. Some of the guys yell at us
to let the fight continue.

"The only reason I'm not breaking your face is because my
number one man is with you," Greg tells me.

"Don't you think this guy has had enough?"

"No. I haven't even started yet."

"Come on," I tell Seth.

"You're not leaving," Greg says as he starts toward us.
Frankie moves to stop him, putting an arm around him and
guiding him away.

I head toward Frankie's car, helping Seth walk.

"Did you come with anybody tonight?"

He shakes his head.

"How'd you get here?"

"I got dropped off."

I remember what his bike looked like last time I saw it. His face sorta resembles that now. I try to open Frankie's car door, but it's locked. He's still over there in the group we just left, talking to Greg.

"How'd this happen?"

"They saw me," Seth says.

I look at him. Droopy eyes and a bloody nose and a mouth that keeps getting smeared the more he wipes it. I think of his reply.

Yeah, they just saw you. It wasn't like you told them off or spit in their face. They simply saw you.

Frankie comes over and unlocks his Toyota.

"Do you have a napkin or anything?" I ask him as we climb inside.

"This is setting up to be no good, man," Frankie tells me. He grabs some napkins out of the glove compartment and gives them to Seth.

"How come?"

"How come? Brandon, man, I'm telling you. Greg is going to find you, and he's not gonna stop next time."

"So I'll keep you with me all the time," I say.

"He almost didn't listen to me tonight."

I look over and see the group of guys still in the parking lot. I wonder where the cops are. They always seem to be around when you don't want them, but they vanish when they're truly needed.

"What'd you say to them anyway?" Frankie asks Seth.

"He didn't say anything," I say, strangely defending a guy I don't even know.

"I told them they're going to rot in hell. Every single one of them."

Frankie and I look back at Seth. Then I glance at the guy driving the car. I know we're both thinking the same thing.

It wasn't what Seth said; it was the way he said it. It didn't sound like a bratty young kid's comment. It sounded like a statement of fact, as if Seth was saying the sky seems overcast tonight. The clouds are thick and, oh yeah, you and your friends are going to rot in hell.

"You might want to avoid saying *anything* to those guys from now on," Frankie says.

"How'd this start in the first place?" I ask Seth. I've barely said ten words to the guy and I'm somehow involved in this mess, so I might as well know why.

"He's been on me ever since last year," Seth says. "Don't know why."

"Greg likes to terrorize people. On the field and off," Frankie says.

"That's gonna get him put in prison," I say.

"Tell me where you live again?" Frankie asks once we're heading toward downtown Appleton. "I forget what street to turn on."

"Just drop me off by the coffee shop. I can walk from there."

"It's seriously no big deal," Frankie says.

"I'll walk."

For a guy who's been helped out a couple of times, Seth sure doesn't sound very thankful. I wonder if he doesn't want us seeing his house again.

There's a silence in the car, and after a few moments I can't take it. I ask him the first question I can think of. "You work anywhere?"

"No."

This isn't just a casual "no." It's the sort of "no" that ends conversations abruptly.

"You should come by Fascination Records sometime," I say. "Where I work."

"I don't buy records."

Frankie shoots me a look.

Yeah, I know. The guy's a little snotty.

We ride in silence until we stop in front of the dark window of the closed coffee shop.

"You don't have to keep helping me out," Seth tells me before he opens the door.

"So you want me to let you get splattered all over the parking lot somewhere?"

"The enemy has only images and illusions behind which he hides his true motives. Destroy the image and you will break the enemy."

"What?" I ask.

Seth opens the car door and starts walking down the sidewalk.

"What'd he just say?" Frankie asks.

"I have no idea."

"I can tell he really likes us."

I laugh. "I keep helping him out, and he keeps acting weird."

"There's a reason he keeps getting beaten up."

"That doesn't make it right."

Frankie drives off. We pass the tall, skinny figure walking in the dark.

"What a strange guy," Frankie says.

"Yep."

"You better watch your back. That's all I'm saying."

31

What are you doing?

It's late and I can't stop thinking of Marvel. Maybe she's up, so I'm trying her on Facebook.

I wait for a while. Ten minutes. Twenty. I wonder what she's doing, whether she's dreaming, or watching television, or simply sleeping.

Listening to music, the reply finally says.

What are you listening to?

My favorites. Ever heard of A Fine Frenzy?

No, I write back.

Love her.

What does she sound like?

She sounds exactly how I feel, Marvel says.

For a moment I have to think about that. **Happy or sad?** I ask.

Yes.

Both? I ask.

Maybe.

Marvel sounds just like herself online. Playful and funny.

I open Spotify and find A Fine Frenzy. It's a woman sing-ing softly. She sounds sad, deep, beautiful. A lot like Marvel seems to be. **I like it,** I tell her.

I picture her in her room, listening to the same song I'm listening to. It's kinda cool, thinking we're together even though walls and miles and the dark night keep us apart.

Do you ever think about what you'll be like ten years from now? she asks.

I never look ahead.

Why?

I'm not sure how to answer. **I don't know. Seems too far off.**

Sometimes I let myself imagine. What might be. What could be.

The song is sad. I almost change it, but I don't. I let it play.

Do you dream a lot? Marvel asks.

Like in my sleep?

Yeah.

Sure.

I think about the conversations I used to have with Taryn, texting or talking on our cells. She'd always be telling me about this girl or that girl, and she'd be complaining and whining. But Marvel is different. She asks me about what life might be like ten years from now and whether I dream a lot.

Sometimes I see myself hovering over a large canvas, as if I'm the painter's brush. The colors change and the picture is so beautiful.

I don't know what Marvel is talking about, but I keep listening.

Sometimes I think I get small glimpses of heaven. Not the kind I can imagine, because what I see is beyond my imagination. Is that crazy?

Yeah, I type. But a cool kind of crazy.

Sometimes I work with clouds like they're pieces of clay. Sometimes I make rectangular shapes out of rainbows. Sometimes I finger-paint poems all over the sky.

I laugh. This girl is definitely crazy. Not sure what to say to that, I answer.

Can you picture it? I don't know—sometimes I think heaven is like that beautiful dream we wake up from and want to go back to. We spend the day longing to fall back asleep in order to see something wonderful again. And one day, when we take that last breath, the dream becomes reality.

All I can think is that I don't want to sleep and I don't want to dream. I just wish I could see Marvel now and talk to her in person.

I'm rambling, she writes.

I like reading it.

I feel comfortable enough to tell you all this. I don't know why.

Something I wanted to say the other day comes to mind. I'm sorry for everything you've gone through.

Yeah, thanks. Me too. I need to go.

I wonder if it's something I said. I didn't mean to bring that up.

It's fine, she writes back. I'm tired anyway and I get wonky when I'm tired.

I love that word. Wonky.

Good night. Maybe I'll see you in my dreams.

Good night.

I know I'll see Marvel in mine.

32

The first thing Mrs. Teed does when I show up with Marvel at their July 4 bash is ask whether she's my girlfriend.

"No, I just work with her," I say as fast as I can.

"What a doll," says the typically animated and talkative Mrs. Teed. "Aren't you looking so pretty today?"

Marvel is wearing a short, lacy dress with a wild pink cotton scarf around her head and neck. She takes off her pink heart-shaped sunglasses. When Mrs. Teed leaves, Marvel laughs.

"I love being called a doll."

"Devon takes after his father," I say.

We soon meet up with Mr. Teed, who barely mumbles a hello. I guess if you lived with someone like Mrs. Teed, you'd stay busy moving around and not say much.

As usual, there is a big spread of food and lots of people. I brought my two brothers with us, and they've already disappeared into the house, doubtless seeking video games. Soon Devon finds us.

"This is Devon, one of the guys," I tell her.

"I've heard lots of good things about you," Marvel says.

Devon shakes her hand like an adult might. "Funny, because I've heard very little about you."

"It's 'cause you're way too curious and you'll only keep asking me more questions," I say to him.

"I love this seventies chic thing you have going on," he tells Marvel.

I laugh. "Since when did you become an expert on fashion?"

"Nobody's claiming to be an expert. I do know what the seventies were all about."

"Devon here knows a little bit about everything," I say.

"What exactly do you know about Thai food?" Marvel asks.

Of all the questions Marvel might ask, this isn't one I could have ever anticipated.

"A lot of people like pad thai, which is fine, but I really like tom yum goong. I like shrimp and mushrooms."

"Impressive," she replies.

"Since when do you like Thai food?" I ask Devon.

He shrugs. "There's a great restaurant downtown that we go to sometimes. Star of Siam."

"I'll have to go there," Marvel says.

She is so confident, and she keeps a genuine smile on her face—the kind even total jerks like Greg would find welcoming. But Greg would like her just because she's good-looking.

"Well, we don't have any Thai food here, but we sure have lots of other kinds. So eat up."

"Thank you," Marvel says.

I'm glad to finally be bringing Marvel around to meet Devon and the rest of the guys. This is the closest I'm going to come to bringing her home. God only knows what Dad would say to Marvel if he saw her. Knowing him, he'd probably be drunk and say some kind of racial slur.

Devon takes off to help his mother. Marvel and I get something to drink and listen to the country music blasting through the speakers.

"He's nice," she says.

I nod. "Yeah, Devon's a good guy. Can be an oddball at times, but he's okay."

"I love oddballs," Marvel says. Her face lights up when she says that.

"I can be an oddball."

"No, you're too predictable."

"Hey," I say.

"That's not an insult. We need people who are tried-and-true."

"That sounds boring."

She raises her eyebrows and takes a sip of her drink. As usual, I wish I could see inside her mind to know what she really thinks.

A couple of hours later we're sitting on some lawn chairs Mrs. Teed gave us, on the edge of the lawn by the road. Just beyond us is a thick cornfield where the fireworks will be set off. We've been sitting here for half an hour watching the sun set and seeing families walk past to look for decent seats for the fireworks.

"Did you used to watch the fireworks in downtown Chicago?" I ask.

"It depended. Sometimes we would be visiting relatives out of state. Or sometimes they would be staying with us. There was always some kind of party going on."

"Like Devon's parents' party?"

"More like some kind of drunken madhouse," Marvel says, staring into the distance. "There aren't too many good memories I can think of. Except for sneaking off with my cousin one July 4 and getting into trouble. Getting into lots of trouble."

I stare at her for a moment and get lost. It's sorta like staring into the west at a beautiful sunset. Except I'm staring at her and she notices.

"Anybody in there?" she eventually asks.

"Yeah, I think so."

"What are you thinking?"

I'm not about to tell her what I'm thinking, because for a moment I was thinking we really make a nice couple. I'm thinking she's really good-looking and she's really sweet, and for some reason she seems to like me. At least a little.

"Nothing," I say.

"Well, you really seem focused on nothing."

Music plays from speakers just down the road where a local band is playing some cover tunes.

"Would you want to go to Lollapalooza with me?"

"You didn't tell me you were going," Marvel says.

"Harry gave me two tickets for Sunday."

"Sunday, huh? Don't you believe in church?"

"Lollapalooza doesn't start in the morning," I tell her.

"Oh, so you'll be going to church, then heading downtown."

I nod. It's a very, very weak nod. "Yeah, sure, maybe."

She laughs. "Maybe I'll think about going. But would you go to church with me?"

"You go around here?"

"I've started going to a small church I found."

"Tell me it's not like five people."

"No. Seven." She laughs.

"But you'll go to Lollapalooza with me?"

"Sure." She doesn't ask who's playing. It doesn't seem like she needs to.

The sun sinks lower, and the sky resembles a darker version of her pink scarf. I don't pay any attention to the hundreds of people around us. For a moment, it feels like we're the only two people out here. This is the way she makes me feel. And maybe that's just Marvel being nice, but it's okay. I need some nice in my life.

I want as much nice as I can get.

The fireworks are better than usual. I know it's because Marvel is sitting next to me. But it's also because they're longer, I think. And they're playing all these great pop tunes to accompany the colorful blasts. It seems like someone knew we were sitting there, so they're playing love songs from popular musicians on the radio.

Then they start the Adele song from the James Bond movie and I suddenly find myself in the movie. Maybe this gives me the courage I need. Maybe this is long overdue.

I don't know. I still don't know if Marvel really likes me or not. I don't know if I'm just the nice guy she works with. But that's okay.

As the reds and blues and whites burst in the sky above us, I stare at the reflection on her perfect face. She looks at peace, and the image is startling because I'm thinking about the flames that took her parents. I still haven't asked her more about it, and maybe I never will. The serenity on her face is scary surprising because I want that same look. I want that same feeling when it's just me staring off into the heavens.

Marvel looks at me and smiles.

There is something there. I know it. There's something in her smile and the way those eyes watch me.

Adele sings about the sky falling and standing together, and all I know is I want to stand next to this girl tonight and tomorrow and the many days after that.

I move my hand over to hers and hold it. Her grip is strong and she doesn't seem to hesitate. She doesn't seem to want to let go.

I stare at the fireworks and listen to the song. I realize I didn't know Marvel Garcia before the start of the summer. But everything can change, just as Artie Duncan found out. We're not promised tomorrow, and we can never predict today. All I know is that Marvel is by my side and I'm not about to let her go.

Marvel pulls her aunt's slightly beat-up SUV to the curb in front of my house and puts it in park.

"Thanks for driving me around," I say.

"Thanks for giving me a reason to."

"I could've walked home like my brothers. But . . . I'm glad I didn't have to."

I see the outline of her face in the darkness. I think and feel a dozen things, all focused on the girl behind the wheel.

"Brandon, I think you're a sweet guy," she says.

No. The helium balloon that's been soaring upward suddenly got popped. "That's like the worst start of a sentence *ever.*"

"It's true."

I groan.

"What? You don't want to be considered sweet?"

"But you just want to be friends," I say.

"We aren't friends?"

I look at her and don't even need to say anything. She knows exactly what I'm thinking.

"I've already told you, I can't," she says. "I just can't get involved. I can—*we* can hang out like this. But we can only be friends."

"You keep saying that," I tell her.

"Because I mean it."

"I just don't understand. . . ."

"You understand a little more," she says.

I take it she's referring to what happened to her parents. How can I even begin to say anything about that?

"It's not like I want something major serious or anything," I tell her.

"I need a friend, Brandon. That is what I really need."

"Okay."

"But that's it. Nothing more. And moments like—like what just happened. You can't do that."

"You didn't let go," I say.

"I know."

"Do you like me?" The question is so third grade I can't believe I let it slip out. But it's there now, like a firework that just went off.

"Of course I do. You know I do. But there are other things—you can't be with me. Not like that."

"I'm not asking for anything—"

"Please," she says, so I shut up.

We stare at each other in the dark.

There are other things.

What are these "other things"? She's already told me about her parents. What else can there be?

"Tonight was great," I say. "Thanks."

"You sound so sad."

"No, this is my 'sweet' voice."

She smiles. "Give me time."

"Time for what?"

"Time to explain everything. Time to figure out a way to tell you."

"Tell me what?" I ask. A car passes us on the street. It's almost eleven o'clock.

"To tell you why."

"Is this about your parents? What happened?"

She nods. "It's about me. It's about what happened between God and me."

Now I'm beyond confused. I want to say more, but I think Marvel is about to cry. Or maybe she already is crying.

"Okay. I'll wait. I'll try to, at least. I'll give you time."

"Thanks," Marvel says.

Everything in me wants to give her a nice little kiss good night. Simply a sweet little kiss. But instead, I just offer a smile and tell her good-bye.

The night is warm and humid. I watch her car drive off and wish I were heading off into the night with her.

I wonder what sort of demons ride with her. I wonder if any await her back at her home.

I know there's always the possibility one is waiting up for me.

Turns out I'm right.

There is a dim light barely worth turning on in the family room. Whenever I walk through the front door and see it on, I tense up. My whole body suddenly turns rigid, and I stop breathing because I know there's the potential of something coming.

"Brandon."

I don't have to wonder anymore. Dad is still in there, and either I woke him up or (God forbid) he's waiting for me.

I move into the room. He's sitting in his regular place in a warped recliner that should've been tossed a couple of years ago. I've thought many times how I'd like to see him die in this chair. They fit each other.

"What are you doing out so late?"

"Watching fireworks." Not that I'm trying to hide anything, but I learned a long time ago it's a bad idea to lie to Dad.

"Who were you with?"

His eyes look like a windshield that's being drizzled on. He's looking at me, but at the same time he looks a little lost. It's somewhere in the middle of this state—scary intense and seemingly incoherent—that Dad can be his most dangerous.

"Just Devon and the guys." Okay, so now I'm lying, but no need to mention Marvel. I don't want him asking questions about her.

"Who was that girl you were with?"

For a moment I wonder what he's talking about. There's no way he could've seen Marvel and me, right?

But Alex and Carter saw me. And they got home some time ago.

"Uh, who?" I play dumb.

"The little Taco Bell lady who works in your store."

Uh-oh.

He's angry. He's got that angry, bitter, biting tone and he's looking square at me.

And when has he ever come into the store?

"I saw you two. You little liar. You little thief."

I have a feeling Dad's the one lying now about having seen the two of us. "She's just a friend."

He laughs, and my skin wants to break out in hives and boils and poison ivy pus.

"They always are," Dad says.

I see a bottle of vodka, another not-so-good sign. He doesn't usually go into the hard stuff unless he's had a "hard" day. Which means the hits are going to be a lot harder too.

"Come over here, you little liar," he says.

I've dreamt of saying no. I've dreamt of making a stand

and fighting back. But he's too big and too strong and too hard.

"Come over here," he says again.

In that ugly, weak light, I can see the pockmarks of acne on his face. Maybe that's what made him so mean. Maybe that's one of the hundred reasons.

"What are you doing with someone like her?" Dad asks. He says it like there's something wrong with her. It's the first time I've ever considered the fact that being with Marvel (which is not what's happening) might be viewed in some kind of negative light.

Dad looks me at me, squints, then picks up the small bottle of vodka and drains it. His eyes dim even more, then he takes hold of the bottle by its top. Suddenly he whips it at my face. It smashes against my skull, and for a moment I black out.

I don't know how long I'm out, but when I finally can open one eye I see him standing over me. I start to cry out, finally releasing the pain I feel in every inch of my body, but he cups a rough hand over my mouth.

"Shut your mouth."

My mouth isn't the only thing that shuts down. Everything seems to shut down. Every single inch of my body.

"You stay away from her. You got that? Her kind only attracts trouble."

I can barely breathe, and I'm almost blacking out again. I nod my head and keep nodding it and I'd keep nodding it for the rest of my life just to get him off of me. Just to make him go away.

"You're going to tell your mother this came from the piece

of trash that girl is living with. The one with the hot rod Trans Am. You got it?"

Again I nod. The vodka bottle didn't break, though it feels like it could've cracked my skull.

"Go put some ice on that and go to your room," Dad tells me as he walks out of the room.

I feel like I'm falling. There is pain, but there's something a lot worse. It's the feeling that a bloody wound keeps getting gashed open time and time again. There's no way it'll ever go away. There's no way it'll ever heal, because some monster is going to keep ripping it open whenever he feels like it, only to scrape away at it. Again. And again. And again.

By the time I'm at the refrigerator I'm shaking so hard I need to hold on to it so I don't collapse. I'm not crying. It's been a while since I've cried when Dad beat me. But I'm shaking violently and I'm bracing for the pain to go away.

I know it's going to be a long time before it does.

35

Somewhere in the middle of the night, the side of my face throbbing with a dull, painful pulse, I have the worst sort of thought a kid can have.

I think about what happened to me and then start thinking about Artie Duncan. Maybe the same anger and rage that gave me a knot on my temple and a black eye ended up killing him.

Maybe the same hands that struck me were the ones that struck Artie.

No, that didn't happen, that couldn't happen.

I wonder what's worse. Killing a complete stranger or bashing your son's face in?

I try to stop thinking this, because there's nothing I can do with it. I don't really think my father is a murderer, but then again, who knows? He could be. I don't know why he would kill someone, but I don't know why he likes hitting me either. I don't understand where the anger comes from, but I do get that it's there. It's there and it's real and maybe, just maybe . . .

Stop.

I think of Marvel telling me about her prayers. I'd like to be able to do that, pray to God. But really, truly, I don't buy it. I don't believe that a prayer I might say is going to do a bit of good. It might make me feel nice for a moment and take my mind off the reality of today, but tomorrow is going to be the same. There's nothing a prayer is going to do to change the monster living with me or the madness he brings. Nothing whatsoever.

So instead of praying, and instead of wondering if that monster is indeed a murderer, I think of Marvel. I want to dream about her.

I want to imagine a shop where I can pick out a dozen different hats for her. A seventies-cool-vibes shop downtown where she holds my hand and smiles and I buy her whatever she wants. Then we walk the city sidewalks and look up at the blue sky and don't have a single care in the world. We're grown up and these dark days are behind us and all we have is each other.

This is what I think about as I drift off toward sleep and unconsciousness. It's a fantasy, but just as much of a fantasy as the prayers Marvel prays.

She can have her dreams, and I'll have mine.

36

Mom is already out the door to work before I get up. It's a good thing, because I look like I was hit by a Metra train. Carter is the first to see me, and he just looks at me with tired eyes as if he's sleepwalking.

"What happened to you?"

"Don't worry about it," I tell him.

"You get into a fight?"

"Does it look like it?"

"Looks like you lost," he says.

"Yeah, sorta does, huh?"

Alex is going to grill me more, I know, but I'll just make up some story. Sometimes I think Alex knows more than he lets on. I see this fear in his eyes, and I try to deflate it because I don't want him suspecting a thing. I'm pretty sure Dad hasn't ever hit the others. Carter is his boy, and Alex he just ignores. But sometimes I see a look and wonder if Alex suspects the truth. So I'll try to stay clear of him for as long as possible.

I cut a couple of lawns before heading over to see Devon. I'm not about to go to the record store, not the way I look. But Devon is the one guy I can hang out with who won't make this into a big deal.

When he answers his door, he lets out a groan and a curse. "That hurts me to look at it," he says.

"Yeah."

I follow him inside the air-conditioned house. I'm still sweaty because I haven't been home since cutting the grass.

"You want an ice pack or anything?"

I shake my head. "Just something to drink."

I'm chugging down some lemonade while Devon just watches me. "One more year," I tell him. "That's it. Then bye-bye."

Devon knows the truth. He guessed after an incident like this. All he managed to get out of his mouth was "Did your father—?" before I interrupted and told him yes. That was all I said, and I asked him to never bring it up again or say a single word about it. Devon promised, and he's kept his promise.

"I'm going to get as far away from here as I can," I say. "Not the town, but him. You know?"

Devon nods but still doesn't say a thing. The guy might be awkward and sometimes dorky, but this is the kind of friend I need. Someone who doesn't feel the need to say something just to talk, because there are times when there's nothing good that can be said. Sometimes you have to just let the silence fill the broken places.

"That eye is gonna be dark for a while," Devon eventually says.

"Got any makeup?"

"I can raid my mother's stash. God knows she wears enough."

I laugh.

"So how's Marvel?" Devon asks.

"Great. I think. Fireworks were awesome."

"Oh, yeah? Did you have fireworks yourself?"

I wince at his corny statement. "Not really. She doesn't want a boyfriend."

"She acts like she likes you."

"Yeah, kind of. I don't know. She's got some tough family issues going on."

"Seems like you guys would make an ideal couple," Devon says.

I laugh. "Yeah, I guess you're right."

"I like her whole art seventies fashion look she's got going on."

"Every day I work with her is a trip because she's always wearing something new and different."

"Since when does Harry need two extra people working with him?" Devon asks.

"He doesn't."

"So, what? You're working for free or something?"

I smile, and Devon realizes he's correct.

"You're a fool."

"You saw her."

"Yeah, but you're still a fool," Devon says. "No girl is worth that."

"Some are."

"Look what happened with Taryn," he says. "Look at all the time and energy."

"Don't remind me."

"So what do you want to do?" he asks.

"How about some Xbox? I'd like to see some blood. Some other people's blood."

We're about to head upstairs when Devon stops me. "Oh, hey, I meant to tell you—they arrested someone for Artie Duncan's murder."

For a moment I feel a little light-headed.

They arrested Dad and he's in jail and now it's all going to come out about the beatings and the nightmare and everything.

"Who?" My voice is weak.

"I don't know—some guy in his twenties. Ordinary guy. They found some incriminating stuff. At least that's what Barton said."

"Barton. Please. You trust him?"

"He overhears stuff."

"Hopefully it's the right guy," I say. Hopefully, for many reasons.

"Bet the guy is a total weirdo, you know?"

"I just want the killer put in jail before the school year starts."

"Yeah, totally," Devon says.

I follow him to his room, ready to empty a gun on whoever I can find on-screen. It's nice to imagine things. Even if it's killing someone.

37

Mom walks by me in the kitchen holding some dry cleaning, then stops, drops it, and turns toward me with a scream. "Brandon!"

She's by my side and suddenly acts like I'm two or something. She's holding the side of my head in absolute horror. It's way too much, but that's Mom. "What happened?" she asks, her eyes the size of apples.

"Nothing." This is a ridiculous comment, and I know it. But that's what boys say to their concerned mothers.

"Brandon Jeffrey, what happened to you?"

"It was a fight."

"Well, I can see that, but who did this and how did it happen? Do you need stitches? Why didn't you tell me about this last night?"

I love when she asks like half a dozen questions all at once, because that means I don't have to answer all of them.

"It's just someone I know. A girl I know."

"A girl did this to you?"

In the other room Carter laughs.

"Shut up or you'll be looking the same way," I shout. "No, not a girl. A girl I know—her uncle did this."

"Why?"

"I guess he didn't like me hanging around with her."

"But why? Here, I have to pick that up."

I go over and grab the dry cleaning off the floor. Mom has just come home from work, and she's still in high heels and a business suit. Dad usually looks like the day after a pub crawl while Mom looks like she's working for Donald Trump. I guess paralegals have to be all dressed up and everything.

She makes me sit and puts together an ice pack for my face.

"The swelling has gone down," I tell her. "Believe it or not."

"This is awful. Did he assault you on the street? Did you see him coming?"

"No. It was just a nice hit with a beer bottle."

See, I'm just tweaking the details some. Changing a vodka bottle to a beer bottle. Changing Dad to Marvel's uncle. It's not *really* lying, right?

Righhhhhhhhhttttttttt.

"I want to know his name, and I want to—-"

"No way. I'm staying away from him."

"We should report this to the police."

"Mom, that's when bad things happen. No, it's fine. It was just a warning. That's all."

"This is *not* fine. Have you seen what you look like?"

"I'm trying not to."

For a moment, Mom exhales. Then I see the tears coming.

"Mom, it's fine. Really, I'm okay. It's okay. I'll stay away from him."

Mom is so tired trying to do her job and keep up with the house. Occasionally she breaks down and cries. I know she's worried about Dad. Well, worried might not be the word for it. More like afraid. Or terrified.

I wonder if he hits you like he hits me.

But I don't think so, because Mom has never asked me, not once. The question I sometimes see in Alex's eyes never shows up in hers. Dad still loves her in his own sick way, I think. I know he keeps things from her, even how much he drinks. But there's no way I can tell Mom what happened. It would destroy her.

"I'll stay away from him," I tell Mom. Then I hug her. I'm not touchy-feely, but occasionally mothers need a hug. "It's going to be okay."

"I'm sorry I didn't see that this morning."

"You leave at six," I say. "I'm not getting up that early."

"I'm sorry I've been so busy."

"Hey, I've been busy too." I smile and try to make a joke and assure her that everything is okay. And for now it is.

The holiday has passed and the wound is going to heal and the anger will probably stay away for a while. They'll forget about this, and I'll bury it in the same place I've buried all those other soul-destroying memories. I put it in a deep, dark well and let it go. I have to. That's the only thing I can do.

38

My phone rings, and I answer even though I don't recognize the number on the caller ID.

"Brandon? What happened to you?"

It's the Monday evening after July 4, and I haven't seen or spoken to Marvel in four days.

"What do you mean?" I ask, as if I have no idea what she's talking about.

"Harry gave me your number."

"Ah, I was guarding that from potential stalkers."

"Are you angry at me?"

"Am I angry at you?" I ask in disbelief.

No, I happen to be angry at my father, but I can't really share that, can I?

"I thought maybe because of what I said . . ."

"No. No, it's not that."

"Then what's wrong?"

I look at the clock; it's almost nine, when the record store closes. "Are you still at the record store?"

"Yes. I actually could've gone home early, but I was just hoping you might stop by."

"Are you calling from your cell?"

"Yes," she says.

"You mean I finally have your number? Watch out, world. It's all downhill from here."

"Stop it," Marvel says.

"So you actually wanted me to come by today, huh?"

"I haven't heard a word from you all weekend."

I know how long it's been. I know how many hours.

"So you actually did want to hear from me?" I ask, teasing with her.

"Stop."

"'Cause you know, the last time we talked—"

"I know."

"I still don't get that. I mean, even Devon said you acted like you're interested in me."

"You're a good friend."

"Oh, that's right," I say. "A good friend. The term every guy wants to be called. 'I was her best friend and watched her walk off with Mr. Right.'"

"Stop it."

"So you totally missed me, didn't you?" I ask.

"I missed some parts. Your sarcasm, I don't know."

A part of me wants to bolt out of the house and get on my bike and meet her in front of Fascination Street Records. But then I remind myself about the purple and orange bruise on the side of my skull.

"Are you coming in tomorrow?" Marvel asks.

"A part of me would like to see you today."

"It's what I said, isn't it?"

"Well, you did sorta say we can't be together. That it has something to do with God and all that."

"Don't make fun of me."

"I'm not. I'm just telling you what I heard."

She's quiet for a moment.

"Marvel?"

"I know how it sounds."

"I just don't get it."

More silence.

"But I don't have to get it," I tell her. "I'm okay with it."

"You're okay with what?"

I think for a moment. My not seeing her has nothing to do with what she told me. It has everything to do with how I look and the truth behind it.

If you want her to tell you the truth maybe you should start by telling her some.

I can feel my heart beating. I don't know if I'm ready for this. I really don't.

"Brandon?"

"Wait there, okay? I'll be there in ten minutes."

"What?"

"Yeah. I just—just wait. I'm ready."

"You're ready for what?"

"For you to know. See you soon."

39

I rush to get there, not because I want to see Marvel so badly (though I do) but more because I know if I don't hurry, I might change my mind. So I pedal as fast as I can and try not to think about what I'm about to do. My heart is beating so fast I can feel the throbbing in my still-swollen temple.

Marvel waits on the curb. She's wearing her hair down without any hat or scarf to accent it. She seems at peace just standing there, waiting. Smiling, she gives me a wave. As I get closer, I see when she notices my face. It's pretty hard to miss the dark welt on the edge of my head like I'm some Frankenstein.

When I finally get off the bike, her mouth is slightly open and she's visibly surprised. More like shocked.

"I know this looks bad, but it's actually a lot worse," I tell her.

"Brandon—"

For a moment I stare at the record store, then look around in all directions. But nobody is around us. There is still some light in the sky, enough to allow her to see the ugly truth.

I just stand, nodding like a fool, needing to get this off my chest. "So I gotta tell you the truth. I thought I'd hide it, but I've been bugging you about personal things and, to be honest, you've shared more with me than I've shared with you."

"What happened?"

I swallow. Hard. "Every now and then, my father likes to throw a punch. It's usually in the stomach, where it won't show. He's a total drunk and a total wreck, and most of the time it's just that. But every now and then . . . well, yeah. This happens."

Someone else might ask why or offer some kind of helpful tip or advice or apology. Marvel just walks over and hugs me. She holds on to me for a while and I almost—almost— feel like I'm going to cry. I'm not going to because I swear I'm incapable of doing it anymore, but I still feel something inside shift. Something that hasn't moved for a very long time.

Marvel doesn't mind hugging me on the corner of Sky Avenue and Second Street. When she finally moves away, I see tears in her eyes.

"Hey, it's okay," I tell her.

She wipes her eyes, then shakes her head as if to say no it's not. Or maybe she's thinking about her own father and her family.

"This still doesn't compare to what happened to you," I tell her.

"People aren't supposed to compare nightmares. They're always equal." She's still examining my bump.

"I look pretty tough, don't I?"

"Thank you."

"For what?"

"For telling me."

I nod. I feel lighter.

"Do you want to walk me home?" she asks me.

"Wow. I get to walk you home?"

"Yeah. But before that, can we just—maybe go by the river? Just to sit for a while?"

"Of course."

Minutes later we've crossed one of the bike bridges and we're sitting on a bench in a gazebo on a small patch of island in the middle of the river. Sometimes people come here to fish. Other times homeless people come to sit in the shade. On this evening, thankfully, we're alone.

For a while Marvel watches the water pass. I think she's going to say something, but she remains quiet.

"I don't want this to change anything," I tell her.

"Change? How so?"

"Well, you know, I don't want you to suddenly feel sorry for me and feel a need to go out with me again."

She shakes her head. "Don't worry."

"Ouch. Maybe you can at least *think* about it."

"Can I just—do you mind if I tell you what I'm thinking?"

I look at Marvel. "When do you *not* tell me what you're thinking?"

"You just shared this thing, and I want to help. That's all."

"Okay," I say.

"The one thing I know—that I believe—is that Jesus sees us for who we are when we go to him. That's what gives me so much strength. Because I come before him with all this stuff. Fears and questions and anger and failure and confusion. He knows."

"Considering what you've gone through, you have a right to ask some questions."

"I have to give him everything because if I don't, it just takes me under. Like someone drowning, you know? That's all I know to do."

"And it works for you, right?"

Marvel nods, then looks at me. "It's the only thing I know that works. It's all."

I glance at the water and see its never-ending motion. "I prefer denial myself. And humor. And deep-dish pizza."

Marvel takes my hand. "I'm sorry, Brandon."

"Yeah, me too. We're both sorry. So what?"

"It matters. I know it does."

I squeeze her hand and look at her. "So okay, I've told you my big secret. Can we agree to tell each other everything?"

"I don't know," she says.

"What? There's more to tell me?"

"I'm not ready," Marvel says. Her voice and face make it seem like she's going to cry again.

"No, don't—come on," I say. "It's fine. Just—whenever you're ready."

"I don't think I'll ever be ready. Not for what's to come."

"And what's that?"

She shakes her head and squeezes my hand back. Then she looks out toward the fading horizon. She doesn't want to say anymore. That's okay. I'll sit here and just be here with her.

She knows and she doesn't care. No, I take that back. She knows and she cares very deeply.

It's a pretty awesome thing.

40

Walking her home feels like it takes forever and then again feels like only a few minutes. We take sidewalks through the center of downtown Appleton and keep walking. We pass the statue of the owl that's the high school mascot. We talk about school next year. I mention how I'm excited about soccer and how much I dislike the football team even though one of my best friends is the quarterback. We talk about cheerleaders, about the fact that I liked one for a while. We shift to music, then on to fireflies. We talk about everything except the heavy stuff.

The conversation seems endless, yet I know that no matter how long it takes, we'll eventually get to her home. Our talk will be over, yet I'll want more.

"Here we are," she says as we arrive at the apartment buildings I've passed a hundred times in my life yet never really noticed.

"Cool."

"I'm in the middle building."

"Okay."

I walk alongside her, guiding my bike beside me as I have the entire way.

"I didn't want you to see where I live," Marvel says.

"Really? Why?"

"Because I thought you might judge me for some reason. Because—because I didn't know you."

"Doesn't matter where you live."

"My uncle and aunt barely make it, so having me there has been a struggle. They don't have any children. I think they tried and couldn't. My aunt has always been like a second mother. Well—that was before I got older, before everything happened with my family. Sometimes she acts like it's my fault. And Uncle Carlos, he definitely isn't a father figure."

I stop for a moment before we get to the parking lot. "Hey—can you promise me something?"

"Depends on what you want me to promise," she says. "I take promises very seriously."

"Will you tell me if your uncle does anything to you? Or even tries?"

She looks at me but says nothing. A car passes by, momentarily lighting us up in the dark night. Clouds have gathered above, shadowing everything, including the two of us.

"Marvel, I want to help."

"What are you going to do? I mean, if something happened? You didn't do anything to your father, did you?"

"He scares me," I say.

"You haven't been around Uncle Carlos."

"I don't know. It's different."

"Why?"

I shrug. I guess my rationale doesn't make sense. I can't even think of striking back at my father. I'd love to, but it just will never happen. At the same time, it doesn't matter how big and bad Uncle Carlos is. I feel protective of Marvel. More protective than I am of myself.

"I'll tell you on one condition," Marvel says.

"What is it?"

"We make a pact. To tell each other if anything happens to either of us."

"Is this going to be a blood pact?"

"Yeah, it'll be a blood pact," she says. "If either of us sheds blood, we tell each other."

"Yeah, okay. Sheds blood or just something bad. You tell me."

"And you tell me."

I reach out and shake her hand. "It's a deal. A pact. A promise."

"I don't want to ask too much of you, Brandon."

"You haven't asked anything."

"Just being here is asking a lot. I know."

There she goes again. "What do you know? Tell me."

"Not tonight. Not now."

"The way you talk, it's like you know the world is going to come to an end or something."

"Or something."

I follow her down a slight hill to the parking lot and over to the middle apartment building.

"Thank you for riding out to see me," Marvel says.

"Thank you for waiting."

She smiles, seems to think about something, then turns around and heads into the building.

I get the feeling she was wondering whether to hug me good night, or maybe give me a peck on my cheek, or maybe just say good night. But she does none of those things. She simply heads into the murky shadows of the place she calls home.

I sigh, knowing I have to go back to a similar place.

Home should never be dark or full of shadows and secrets. It should be bright and full of open doors. It should be full of stories wanting to be told.

I'm glad I've told somebody one of those stories I didn't think I could ever tell. I just hope there won't be any more of them. From either of us.

41

A few days later I get a Facebook message from Frankie. **Hey man, check this out.**

I go to the link he sent. A picture pops up on my laptop, and at first all I can see is the word LOSER written on something.

*That's not on something. That's on some*one.

I see the name Seth Belcher. Someone wrote in black ink on his forehead. In the picture it looks as though he's been crying.

What happened? I message Frankie.

Looks like they were messing with him again. I don't know how or when.

I can feel the anger building inside of me. **I'm going to go to his father.**

Sgt Packard?

Yeah, I type.

I wouldn't.

This is gonna go on all summer.

Yeah.

Frankie's indifference annoys me almost as much as the picture I'm seeing. **You know it was Greg, don't you?**

Yeah, I'm sure.

I think about going to the police station, then realize I can't. They'd ask me about my shiner and I'd have to lie. Nope. Can't do anything about this for a while.

Maybe go find Seth. See if I can help him.

You remember where the guy lives? I ask Frankie.

Yeah, just came from his house a minute ago.

Shut up.

Have no idea. It was dark when he led us to that dead-end street.

Is that a pun?

A what? Frankie asks.

Never mind.

I head out, ready to cut some lawns and make some money. I might make it back to the record store. I realize that black eyes take a long time to go away. My bruise keeps evolving into a rainbow of strange colors. I'd rather not have to explain it to Harry, who will surely ask.

Maybe I can find Seth and he'll realize I can sympathize with him.

The third time I see the car, I know someone is following me.

I don't recognize it, and the first couple of times I saw it didn't make me think twice. But the third time I see the black Jeep Cherokee with tinted windows, I know it's following me. It has to be, since it's just parked on the curb half a block down from where I'm cutting my third lawn of the day. No one gets out of the SUV. It just sits there and waits.

I wipe sweat off my forehead as I put my lawn mower back in the trailer. I decide to walk by the parked car. Maybe I'll be able to see who is inside. Maybe the person inside has something to say to me.

I step up to the sidewalk and walk past two houses before the SUV pulls away. It doesn't start up and squeal its tires and take off. It just moves away.

For a moment I wait to see if it's going to come back, but it doesn't. I text Marvel. **Does anybody in your family drive a black Jeep Cherokee?**

No. Why?

I'll explain why when I talk to her next. Which I hope will be tonight.

I never do get hold of Marvel that night, or the next day.
I realize something is up when Harry calls to say he needs me
to come in. "She called in sick yesterday and again today."

I suddenly feel ill, imagining the worst. "What'd she say?"

"Just she's got some stomach bug."

"I can be there within the hour," I tell Harry.

First I need to see if I can talk to Marvel. Or better yet, see
her in person.

After texting and calling, I borrow Glyn's truck and drive
over to her apartment building. I text her again to say I'm at
her building and need to see her. I finally get a call back.

"Are you okay?" I ask before I even hear her voice.

"Yes, I'm fine."

"What's going on?"

"Nothing. I just can't work today."

"You don't sound like you have the stomach bug."

"It's my aunt. I didn't want to go into details with Harry."

"What's wrong with her?"

There is a pause.

"Marvel?"

"I can't tell you."

So much for the pact.

"What about the promise we made to each other? About saying if something happens to one of us?"

"Nothing happened to me," Marvel says. Her voice is calm, probably more calm than mine.

"Then what's going on?"

"I can't tell you."

"Is this like female stuff? My mother will sometimes tell us boys to not worry about something because it's female stuff."

Her laugh makes me feel better. "No, it's not 'female stuff.' It's more complicated than that."

"I'm standing outside your apartment building."

"I can't leave my aunt. You just have to trust me on this."

"Marvel, I don't—"

"Brandon, please."

I glance around the parking lot, wondering if her uncle might be around, ready to drive into me with his car.

"The last thing I need after the past couple of days is pressure. Please."

I sigh. "Okay, sorry. All right. But just—just let me know if I can do anything."

"Just trust me when I tell you I'm okay."

I head back to the truck. I don't know if I believe her when she says she's okay, but I have to let her be. I hate it. It's like Seth. I want to help him out, even though I barely know him, and even though he doesn't seem to care for my help.

"Keep in touch," I say.

"I'll see you soon," Marvel says.

43

For some reason I'm having a hard time sleeping, so I decide
to ride my bike.

But it's about two in the morning, isn't it?

I go riding, even though I don't have a light on my bike.
I head down to the record store, and it's totally lit up inside.
I wonder if Harry forgot to turn off the lights when he closed.
Then I see that the front door is open, and strange music is
coming from inside.

I hear my voice being called out as if it's part of the song.

But that doesn't really make sense, does it?

"Brandon . . . ," the voice says.

It's Marvel's voice. She says it in a desperate way, a plead-
ing fashion. She sounds tired and wounded.

"Brandon, help me."

I get off my bike and go inside the store. The music is
louder, and it gives me the chills. It sounds like a church
organ playing a weird, somber tune, the kind you might hear
at a funeral. Then I see Marvel dressed in black.

"You came when I called," she says.

But she never called, and why is she dressed in black?

"Am I dreaming?" I ask.

"Doesn't reality sometimes seem like a wonderful dream or a horrible nightmare?"

"Yes."

"Life can be that way if we allow it to be," Marvel says.

So am I making up these images and words and playing them out in my head?

"Are you okay?"

"Yes. But you aren't and neither are any of the people around you."

"Why is that?"

"Because something bad is coming. Something very bad."

The organ suddenly stops playing and the silence feels really eerie.

"This is a dream," I say.

Marvel shakes her head and begins to laugh. "No, Brandon. This is definitely *not* a dream."

Then I see her face morph into my father's hateful glare. "Come over here, Brandon," he says in that tone I know so well.

Now I don't want to be dreaming anymore. I want to wake up.

"You think you can go behind my back but you can't, son. You can't and you never will."

Suddenly the figure in black starts running toward me, but it's not my father. It's Seth Belcher, and he looks very dead and very cut up and very creepy.

I start running, and I'm running and I think I actually

try to run out of my bed. I jerk and pinch my neck and then realize I'm almost off my mattress. I'm sweating and my heart is racing.

For a long time, I just breathe in and out. I can't remember the last nightmare I had. Most of the time I don't get crazy dreams. The world is crazy enough without them. This came out of nowhere.

Then again, so did Marvel.

44

"Did you hear the latest on the search for Artie Duncan's killer?" Harry asks.

His question surprises me. "I heard they let the suspect go, right?"

"Yeah. The cops are telling teens in particular to be on the alert. They don't think Artie's death was random. They feel it was premeditated and well planned out. That's why they're having such a hard time finding who did it."

"Did the police say who the suspect was?"

"You need to be careful," Harry says without answering. "I know you ride your bike around, sometimes at night, so just be careful."

I think of the odd nightmare I had the other night. Harry's gaze seems serious. I know he's trying to both encourage me and warn me.

"Tell your friends, too," he says.

"You really think there's some crazy killer out there?"

His eyes dart around behind his glasses. "I pray there's not,

Brandon. I'd like to think Artie's death was just some random, awful act of violence. But you can never be too careful in this world. I hear about kids being abducted all the time. It makes me not want to let our boys out of the house."

"Yeah, it's freaky."

For a moment he stares at me. "You know—you can tell me stuff if you need to."

"About Artie's death?" I'm not sure I'm following him.

I think about Devon buying pot from Artie and what this all means. There's no way Harry knows about this. Right?

"No, just about anything." He points to his temple, and then I get what he's referring to.

I told Harry I'd fallen off my bike. It wasn't a very convincing lie, and I hadn't worked very hard to sell it when I told him.

"Thanks."

That's all I say. I'm not going to tell him what's happening at home.

Harry's the kind of father I wish I had. The kind who cares.

The world would be a much better place if everybody had a father like that.

45

The worst part about telling somebody something deeply personal is wondering later whether you said too much.

I can't help thinking this, because I haven't spoken much to Marvel since I told her the truth about my father. She's been in at the record store a couple of times, but we haven't talked about anything deep and meaningful. Now I'm wondering if I should have said anything.

Dad is ignoring me, the way he always does after an "incident." This seems to be the way he copes. It's better for him not to talk to me, because I remind him of what he did. Mom has mentioned Marvel's uncle to me several times, reminding me to avoid being around him.

One weeknight after reluctantly telling Marvel good-bye, I ask if we can talk on the phone once we both get home. She calls me right away.

"That was fast," I tell her.

"The apartment is empty. My aunt and uncle should be coming home any minute. You wanted to talk?"

"Yeah, I just—I feel stupid about some of the things I told you."

"Why? There's no reason you should."

I'm not exactly sure why. I'm embarrassed about it, but I also feel as though something between us is different now. And not different in a good way.

"I know you better now," Marvel says. "That's a good thing."

"Really? I think it was easier talking with you at the store when you didn't know so much."

"You know stuff about me."

"Not everything. Like what's going on with your aunt."

"What if I told you everything?" she says with a bit of humor laced in her tone. "Just wrote it all up and delivered it in one sitting? How boring would that be?"

"Not boring. I'd understand you more."

"So why do you need to understand me?"

I don't say anything.

"I understand why, Brandon. I think I do. But you know my thoughts on the two of us. There can't be anything like that. Do you want to get to know me because you're generally curious about my life, or is it because you think it's going to help you start dating me?"

Her honesty is pretty incredible. And pretty much on target, too.

"Maybe both," I say. "I'm trying to be honest like you are."

"Things would be so much easier between us if you took that out of the equation. The whole guy-girl thing. Both of our lives are already complicated enough. And there's just so much . . ." This time she doesn't finish her thought.

"There's just so much what?" I ask.

"There's just too much that I could say."

"About what?"

She doesn't answer.

"About the guy-girl thing?" I ask.

"No. About the whole issue of faith. That whole area. That's something I'm dealing with daily. And it's heavy."

"What? Why?"

"Because every day I doubt the things I know and believe."

Sometimes it feels like I'm talking about the color blue when she's actually talking about purple. Somehow this girl makes me color-blind.

"You don't seem to have doubts," I tell her.

"Oh, if you only knew. It's bad sometimes. And I scream out to God to give me peace and comfort. But he doesn't always do that, does he?"

"No." I say this, but I don't really know. Not for sure.

"I keep praying for a miracle. That's all. I ask God for one, but it never comes."

"What kind of miracle?"

"I don't know. Any kind. Just one. I know and believe, but I still ask him for one."

I'm about to ask her to explain this more, but suddenly I hear something in the background shuffling around.

"My aunt and uncle are home. I have to go."

"Okay."

"More on that later," Marvel says.

"More on miracles and all that?"

"Sure. That and more. Bye."

She's gone before I can say another word.

I wonder what she means by saying she wants a miracle. She's probably one of the most outspoken people about faith I've known, though the crowd I hang around with doesn't have those kinds of people in it. There are kids at school whose whole lives seem to revolve around church. They're always talking about youth group and mission trips and raising awareness for one cause and helping out people with another. And all of that is great, but sometimes those people wear me out.

It wears you out 'cause you don't really buy into it.

That's the truth. I don't know if I'd tell Marvel that in so many words, but it's the truth.

Getting me to have the sort of faith she has. Now *that* would be a miracle. But that's not gonna happen.

46

It's strange that I find myself thinking so much about two people I didn't even know at the beginning of the summer. Marvel, of course, and also Seth Belcher. Today I got a message from Frankie saying he found out Seth's actual address. I didn't know he was looking for it. It didn't seem like Seth mattered to him. But this is why I love Frankie. He'll surprise you. No big deal, just here, take this address.

I borrow Glyn's truck and plug the address into my phone's GPS. It takes me to a very different place from where Seth had us drop him off that night—past Randall Road in Glenforest Estates. I wonder if Frankie got this wrong. Seth has never struck me as being well-off.

I pass the road that leads to Taryn's house. I'm not looking forward to school starting, because I'll have to see her daily. It'll be painful. Especially if I happen to be hanging around Marvel. My relationship with Taryn seems like a whole lifetime away.

The GPS leads me to a large two-story house that looks

fairly new. I park on the street, then get out and look around for the black Jeep Cherokee. I haven't seen it again, but I keep looking out for it. Just in case. Not that I'd know what to do if I saw it.

I knock on the door, totally not expecting Seth. But when the door opens, it's his face I see. I probably look as surprised as he does.

"Hey, Seth."

"Hey."

"Is this your house?" I can't help asking the obvious, but I'm still a little thrown off.

"Yeah."

"So that night—the place we dropped you off . . ."

"It was a friend's place."

I think of the street with a couple of deserted houses and the small, run-down house with the dim front light. What kind of friend might that be?

And since when does this guy have friends?

"So, uh, you busy?"

He looks behind me in both directions, then shakes his head. I can tell he's nervous.

"I'm by myself," I say.

"Okay."

I'm not sure what to say, since I swear I didn't think he'd be here. "I figured I'd just see what's going on."

"Just playing Xbox."

I nod. He doesn't seem to be even thinking about inviting me in.

"What happened to you?" He asks if Greg and his buddies had anything to do with my fading black eye. The names he uses to describe Greg and his buddies would get him beaten up again.

"It wasn't them. It was something else."

"I'm starting to take mixed martial arts. Five days a week."

This sounds like a bad joke, but I can tell Seth is being serious. "Well, that's good."

"One of these days, when someone tries to grab me from behind, I'll be ready. The only problem is when they weigh more than you."

Seth might be 150 pounds if he's lucky. Greg is definitely over 200.

"Yeah, or if they happen to play football and are stupid."

He doesn't laugh with a "that's funny" laugh but more of a "that's a cute joke" sort of chuckle.

What am I doing here? Really?

"Have you seen any more of those guys?" I ask.

Seth just shrugs as if he doesn't know what I'm talking about. I'm feeling pretty stupid.

"Look—Seth—can I give you my number? I just want to help out. I hate Greg and the guys he hangs around with."

"I can take care of myself."

Yes, clearly you can.

"Yeah, I know," I tell him. "Just—can I just give you my cell?"

"Sure. Wait a sec."

Seth closes the door, then he opens it again, holding his large smartphone. I give him my number and he types it in.

"Now I know who to call instead of 911."

"Yeah, if you need something," I tell him.

An awkward moment passes, so I nod and tell him I'll see

him later. But even this doesn't get a nice "See ya" in reply. Seth just shuts the big door of his big house without saying a word.

Maybe I shouldn't be trying to help this guy out. Maybe some people don't want help.

Maybe this kid is getting exactly what his attitude deserves.

47

Marvel greets me with a smile. The day has suddenly become brighter despite the storm clouds outside.

"You're back," I say as I scan the room to see who else is around.

"Of course."

"Love the beret," I tell her.

"I found it this past weekend. Do you like going to thrift stores?"

"Not really. But I'd go with you."

"Maybe we can find you some interesting clothes," Marvel says.

"I'm not dressing in anything seventies."

"You could use some color. And something that doesn't have a Nike or Adidas logo on it."

I listen to the song that's playing and know Harry didn't pick this album out. "Who is this?"

"Sara Groves. She's a Christian artist."

I nod. "Harry let you put this on?"

"He can't resist someone in a red beret."

Yeah, especially when that someone is you.

"These songs fill me with hope. It's tough enough starting the day on your own. It's great to have some companions in the ongoing war."

"Well, I'd be your companion."

"You already are," Marvel says.

She surprises me by saying this, but I guess I shouldn't be so surprised. Maybe I just need to believe it.

I've been at the record store three hours, and it's actually busy. Harry's had me helping him with a large display in one corner. A poster falls down, and Marvel and I have to put it back up. An older woman talks to me for a long time about the band Rush.

It's around one in the afternoon when Marvel stops for lunch. I want to go out with her, especially since this is one of those days when I don't think I'm getting paid. But she starts to head out without asking me. I get the idea she simply wants to be on her own.

"Hey, Rush man, why don't you take lunch too?"

I look over at Harry, who has a big smile on his face.

"Yeah, come on with me, then," Marvel says.

I love being treated like some twelve-year-old boy around here. But I follow Marvel and don't really mind.

We go to a small deli in the library that Marvel says she loves, then take our food and sit in the small park behind it.

"I like coming here because you feel like this little park is just your own," Marvel tells me as she unwraps her sandwich.

"Nobody ever seems to come here, at least not when I'm here."

The gray clouds above us don't look like they're going to rain, but they're still thick and not letting the sun shine through. I nibble on my turkey sandwich.

"I went to see Seth Belcher today, the kid I told you about who's been bullied."

"Yeah? What for?"

I laugh. "Yeah, he was wondering the same thing. Felt like a total idiot."

"But why did you go see him? Did he even know you were coming?"

"No. I just showed up. Was hoping for a way to get to know him, let him know there's help. I gave him my phone number."

"I'm sure that just made his day."

"Ouch," I say. "I'm just trying to help."

She gives me a knowing, complicated look that takes me off guard.

"What?"

Marvel swallows her bite of sandwich. "I agree. That's just what you do. You just try to help."

"Is that a bad thing?"

"No. Not at all."

"I don't always," I say. "I stay out of trouble. At least, I have until this summer. For some reason."

"It's been a different summer. Probably for everyone around here."

I just nod, but I want to ask her how she feels about her parents and how she manages to cope. I want to ask her whether her faith really, truly is real and whether she can offer a little bit of it to me, like sharing a bag of chips. I want her to explain how she can be so happy when it seems like so many things in her life are sad. I want to know how a guy like me can get a girl like her to fall for him. Not in a passing "you're cute" sort of way, but in an "I'll die for you" kind.

"I bet you can't wait for school to start," she says.

Only if you're standing there on opening day next to me.

"I'm eager to finish high school," I tell her.

"Yeah."

"There—right then. I saw it."

"What?"

"This look you get sometimes. It comes at least once a day every time we talk."

"What look?"

"It's like—it's sad."

"I'm sorry."

"Don't be. I just want to know why. You've been in a good mood all day."

"I don't mean to look a certain way," Marvel says.

I try to remember what I said. To see what might have made her mood suddenly change.

"You don't want to finish high school?"

"No, it's not that," Marvel says. "I'd very much like to finish high school."

"You say that as if you think you're not going to finish high school."

She smiles but doesn't say anything. "I need to use the restroom. Do you mind?"

"Marvel?"

"No, it's just—I'm sorry."

I watch her walk across the mulch of the park and up the steps to the library. I suddenly feel like a fool, which seems to happen a lot when I'm around Marvel and talking.

I sigh and look up at the sky. And that's when I see it.

A beam of light suddenly pierces through the sky as if I'm watching some kind of movie or animation. It's like a hole suddenly burns into the gray ceiling above me, allowing a bright burst of golden yellow to shine down like some kind of celestial spotlight.

I blink, then look again. It's still there. I squint and stare and it's still there. It doesn't look real. I've seen amazing rainbows and sunsets and even stars at night, but this is unreal. I've never seen anything like it.

I watch it for a moment and can't wait for Marvel to see it. I hold my breath, hoping for her to come back.

But it disappears as quickly as it showed up, just as Marvel returns.

"What?"

I stand and keep looking. It's like some bad joke. Or like I'm dreaming this. "Did you see that?" I ask her.

"What?"

"The sky. Did you see that? It was like the sun was shining in this one spot. It was really cool."

"No," Marvel says as she sits back down.

I keep looking up, waiting and watching.

"You okay?" she asks me.

"No. Man, you should've seen it."

Maybe I'm losing my mind. Maybe for some reason, I'm really starting to lose it. And maybe Marvel's the cause.

48

Devon is at it again. Playing police detective or Sherlock Holmes or something.

"Where are we going?" I ask after riding in his car for ten minutes.

"Somewhere."

"I told you I didn't want to get Sonic," I say.

"We're not going to Sonic. Even though I do believe their drive-through system is the best thing in the world of fast-food restaurants."

We're headed toward the center of Appleton.

"Is something happening in town?"

"Nope."

We head over the bridge and turn left onto Rush Street. When we get to an old industrial building Devon slows down.

"Are you going to kill me or something?" I joke. Probably

not the best kind of joke, considering what happened to
Artie.

"No. Just—here, I'm going to keep driving, then turn
around and park on the street."

"What for?"

"I keep telling you, wait."

So we sit in his Jeep, waiting. Every time I try to talk,
Devon hushes me. I wait and yawn and move around in my
seat.

"There—lean down a bit," Devon tells me.

I sink down in the leather seat as I see the twin lights of a
vehicle heading toward us, then turning into the abandoned
parking lot of the equally empty warehouse. The car—some
kind of big town car—parks and goes dark. We wait some
more. I can't see if anybody got out of the car since we can
barely see that far in the murky night.

"Look at the warehouse," Devon says. "Just beyond it."

I see the outline of an old smokestack behind the warehouse. Not sure what it was used for or if it has anything to
do with the building or the river. Then I see the side of it light
up, as if a spotlight is shining on it.

I see the words LETON lit up—the APP doesn't show
from where we sit.

"What's going on?" I ask in a whisper.

"I don't know. But I followed that car here the other night.
Belongs to Otis Sykes."

I remember the old, expressionless driver passing me as
I left the quarry. It could have been the same car.

"What's he doing here?"

"He or someone is doing some work. The lights in the

warehouse go off. Then later on I see the smokestack actually working."

"What do you mean working?" I ask.

"Like billowing smoke."

"Maybe he wants to just, like . . . run a smokestack?"

Devon doesn't even smile at my attempt at humor.

"How'd you know he'd be here again?"

"I've come two other nights and he's been here."

It doesn't look *that* sinister. "So what's that have to do with anything?"

"You tell me," Devon says. "Something is going on with Otis Sykes. I don't know if it has anything to do with Artie Duncan, but who knows?"

"The cops obviously know about him. I'm sure they're keeping an eye on him."

"Don't you think this is a little weird?"

"I think it's weird you sleuthing around like this," I tell him.

Then again, Devon always seems to have a new hobby or a strange fascination.

"You don't think this guy suddenly coming here out of the blue is a bit odd?"

"Of course. But I'm having an odd summer."

"Mrs. Duncan told someone that Artie liked walking by the river late at night. What if he stumbled into something here? And then one thing led to another."

"The cops say Artie wasn't just killed. That it was a planned thing," I argue, repeating what Harry told me. "Someone *wanted* to do that stuff to him."

"But what if it was done to look that way?" Devon asks, his voice still in a low whisper.

"You still think this has something to do with the pot Artie was selling?"

"I think it's tied somehow. Yeah."

I turn to get a little more comfortable in the seat. "So what do you want to do? Keep spying around until we end up the same way?"

"That's why I'm showing you. I figured you'd have some idea."

"My idea is we tell a cop."

"Yeah?"

"Yeah, totally. I don't want to have anything to do with the Artie Duncan thing. Seriously. I got enough to worry about."

"But what—we just call up the police, or do we go in and see someone?"

"What about Mike Harden? The cop who came to our school?"

We keep watching out the window. The car's lights have gone off now.

"You really think we should tell them?" he asks.

"Yes. And I really want to stop sneaking around like this. It's going to start giving me nightmares." Even though they seem to have already arrived.

"I'm not going to the police by myself," Devon says.

The car starts up again and turns down the street away from us. Devon and I wait a minute, then head back down the road, passing the warehouse. I try to see if there's anything odd about it, but nothing stands out.

"I'll go with you," I say. "You get hold of Harden and let me know, and I'll be there."

"What are you going to say?"

"I'm just going to listen to you talk. This is your thing."

"We might be onto something here."

"I really hope we aren't."

A car comes toward us down the street, and I catch a tiny glimpse.

"What the—" I start to say.

"What?" Devon asks.

I turn around in my seat to see where the passing car is headed.

"It's nothing," I say. I feel a falling sensation, the sort of feeling I get when I know my father is waiting for me at home.

The car that just passed was a black Trans Am. Just like the car Marvel's uncle drives.

49

Are you okay?

I send this text and then wait a long time. I think I'm just a bit shaken up from my trip with Devon and from seeing the car belonging to Marvel's uncle pass us. At least Dad wasn't up when I got home.

Yep.

That's all I get. A yep. Not even a yes. I want more than a yep.

I wait for a while until I'm thinking about shutting the phone off and trying to sleep. But then I hear the glorious sound of another text coming through.

Are YOU okay?

I look at her question. I breathe in. I think, and then I start typing and stop thinking.

No, I'm not, thank you very much.

What's wrong? she asks.

Everything.

Like what?

Again I don't hesitate. I'm tired of all this, this waiting. This wondering. This whole worrying about Marvel this and that.

I'm tired of thinking about you. There. I said it.

No you didn't, she says.

What?

Well, technically, you texted it.

I stare at her text, then crack up.

Do you think you're the only one? she asks.

The only one what? I type.

You are always on my mind, Brandon. I pray for you often.

I'm about to say what I'm thinking, which is something like *I want more than your prayers* or *I'm not sure I want your prayers*, when she says more.

I pray that I do what I'm supposed to do.

Okay, here she goes again.

Is that stay away from me? I ask.

It's not about staying away from you. It's about not falling for you. Those are two different things.

She makes it sound like she actually might fall for me. Like that's a bad thing.

Or maybe possibly that she already has.

I want you to fall.

Silence.

Is it SO bad to fall?

More silence.

Now I *really* want to turn my phone off or simply toss it in the Fox River. I wait. I try to remember if I grew this frustrated with Taryn.

It's not frustration, it's confusion.

Are you there? I type.

It feels like the clock just starts to nod asleep on the wall, taking its sweet time before it starts ticking again. I sigh and stare at my phone.

Yes, I'm here.

I thought you went to bed, I type.

I'll be here for as long as I can be, Brandon. I wish you knew that. I wish there was a way for you to see that. I really do.

As usual, I'm lost, I tell her.

One day you won't be. I promise. Good night. Need to climb quickly off this ledge.

And just like that, she's gone. Again.

50

These are the things I picture in my dreams. This time I know I'm in my bed asleep, deep in Slumberland. But I can see everything in the most clear, vivid way.

I see a shadow in the dark walking—no, he's dragging something. Someone. A body. I'm not in front or behind him, nor am I some ghost hovering. It's more like a movie. Some horror movie I'm watching.

What is going on here?

Then I hear the crack of a gunshot and feel the shot against my side and hear my voice scream out in pain even though I'm not hurting anymore.

Am I dead?

The clouds move and shift and I see a million stars above, then a rainbow forming and the sunlight fading, just like my vision.

This is a dream, but it feels real and it feels right in some sick sort of way.

I see a large plume of black smoke coming from a

smokestack and flames rising to the horizon. I hear screams and cries. Awful, hellish sort of cries.

I move and jerk and try to get out of here, to force myself awake. But I can't leave. I can't do a thing.

Then I see a figure—the same figure as the one dragging the body in the woods?—with a mask over most of his face and some kind of hood over his head. The eyes stand out because they look like angry red embers.

It's a killer and he's out to terrorize the town and he's just started with Artie Duncan.

Then I see another figure and know it's Marvel coming toward me. Rushing, running from somewhere, calling out. But I'm falling, I'm drifting away.

I hear her calling out my name, and I keep waiting for her to at least hold me one time before I'm finally out. But I never feel her touch or see that sweet smile.

I wait, and wait, and then open my eyes and see I'm still waiting in my bedroom.

51

I'm getting used to these hideous and painful things happening to me, then waking up the next day and going on as usual. Maybe that's not normal, but I don't know what you're supposed to do. In a movie there's some kind of big standoff, but this is my life and the standoff would have to be with my father. So I do all I know how to do: I just keep going.

So the day after the weird nightmare of creepy things, I keep going. It doesn't even faze me. Being beat up by your father gets you down. Nightmares, not so much.

Morning comes and it's time for work, both the kind I get paid for and the kind I don't (but that comes with perks). I don't tell anybody, including Marvel, about the nightmares. Who knows what she would say. Knowing her, she'd probably tell me she's seen the same things and has a totally logical explanation for them. Then she'd tell me she can't tell me what it is.

I'm busy, and the days pass by quickly. Nothing else comes along. No creepy dreams and no late-night drives with Devon. He hasn't spoken to the police yet, and I'm not going to push him to. Nobody else is found dead, and so far Marvel and I have nothing to report to each other. I keep looking forward to the first Sunday in August, when we will go to Lollapalooza.

Yet as each day goes by, something seems to weigh over me. Maybe it's just the reality of living with a man who would slap a bottle against my forehead. Maybe it's just wondering how long Marvel will continue to tell me she can't be with me. Or maybe it's this constant fear that something bigger is happening that I can't see or know about, but is happening nonetheless. Something that involves Marvel and myself and my father and her uncle and Artie Duncan and everybody else. Some kind of awful terror I can't even begin to imagine.

Or maybe—and this might be even worse—I have started imagining it. Even though I have no idea why.

52

"Do you believe God talks to people? Like literally talks to them?"

Marvel's question comes out of nowhere, almost like God is asking it. I'm a bit freaked out, to be honest. And this shouldn't surprise me. Not this sort of question from her.

The Cure is playing in the background. Harry is around but nowhere to be seen.

"I'm being serious."

Marvel is holding some new T-shirts in her hands. I'm wondering what prompted her question.

"I . . . guess," I say in the weakest sort of way.

Marvel throws the T-shirts at me. I pull away the one hanging off my head and then look at her to see if she's teasing or angry. She looks somewhere in between.

"What?" I ask. "What'd I say?"

"I spend so much time waiting to ask you something, and then I get—that."

"You get what?"

"*That.*"

"I'm sorry."

She comes over and picks up the T-shirts that fell to the floor. "You're just being honest."

"I'm still sorry."

I give the last one back to her. It's a Grateful Dead T-shirt.

"Should I even try to ask why?" I say.

"No."

She walks off. Next time I'll fake whatever the response should be.

Marvel will see right through it.

Later, before the day is over and I'm left with a hundred things I wish I'd said, I apologize for my earlier reply.

"It's fine. I shouldn't have asked that."

"Why?" I say. "You can ask me anything. I want you to ask anything."

"No, maybe it's not that. I shouldn't have expected a certain kind of response. That's where I went wrong."

"I'm sorry to be flippant about stuff like that."

"You're being yourself. And I like that."

"Even if myself can be a moron."

"I like that moron," Marvel says. "Sometimes. Most of the time."

"Enough to still go to Lollapalooza with him?"

"If you'll go to church."

I nod. "I'll go anytime—doesn't have to be just that Sunday."

"Okay. Sounds good to me."

I suddenly realize I need to ask Mom about the concert. Dad—yeah, I'll pass on asking him. I might have to make something up for Mom.

I get another idea.

"Hey—the Superman movie—did you ever see it this summer?"

Marvel shakes her head.

"It's playing at the cheap theater tonight. Any interest?"

She grimaces.

"Wow," I say. "Ouch. That hurts."

"I'm making that face 'cause of the film."

"It's not that bad."

I remember seeing it and thinking it was pretty bad. But I'll try anything to get her to hang out with me.

"It's not a date," I say, raising my hands at the word *date*.

"Of course not. Just two people going to see *Man of Steel*. Right?"

"Exactly. No interested parties. Just friends."

"Too bad I don't have a bike to ride."

I laugh.

Wow, she's full of zingers today.

"You really know how to make a guy feel special."

Marvel heads toward the back room.

"I can drive my neighbor's truck," I say.

"How romantic," she calls back at me.

53

I expect Marvel to say she's coming down, but instead I get buzzed upstairs. I didn't hear a voice, and I wonder if it's Marvel who actually buzzed me. After going up the stairs and finding number 33 on the third floor, I barely knock before the door opens and a woman gives me a grim stare.

"Oh, I'm sorry," I say, starting to walk away.

"Are you here for Marvel?" She has a thick Spanish accent and is short and slender with a hard, square face that reminds me of a hammer.

I nod.

"I'm Rosa, her aunt," she says, offering her hand to shake. She might be in her thirties, or maybe early forties.

In one way I can totally tell that this is Marvel's aunt. Yet in another way, she couldn't seem more different from the girl I'm here to see. Rosa's got her hair up and a lot of makeup on, and she's wearing a dress and heels. She looks like she was pretty once, but something about her seems tough. Like somehow all the soft and fun parts about this woman were scraped off years ago.

She doesn't move away from the doorway. I get the idea she doesn't want me to come in, though I wonder why she wanted me to come all the way up here.

"You're the boy she's been seeing a lot of, aren't you?"

I realize I didn't even say my name. "Yeah. I'm Brandon."

"Brandon what?"

I can see muscles in the woman's neck as though she works out quite a bit.

"Brandon Jeffrey."

Rosa glances back over her shoulder, but keeps the door halfway closed as if to make sure I can't look inside.

"She will be coming out in a minute," Rosa says.

"Thanks."

"Do you go to high school?"

I nod. "I'll be in Marvel's class this fall."

"Oh." The way Rosa says this makes it sound like she's surprised. And disappointed.

"You do know she probably won't be there for the whole school year, right?"

"No." I'm genuinely surprised to hear this.

"We're probably going to move," she says with her strong accent. "It looks very good like we will."

I'm about to say something when Rosa moves and opens the door.

"Hi," Marvel says.

She moves past her aunt as if to make sure I don't linger. "I won't be too late," she tells her aunt.

"Nice to meet you," I say as the door closes.

I think about what Aunt Rosa said and wonder if it's true. Maybe this is what Marvel has been hinting about. Maybe this is why she can't get serious and have a boyfriend.

Or maybe Aunt Rosa is saying that for some other reason.

I decide to not say anything about Rosa's comments. For now.

The date that's not really a date is fine. The movie is over-the-top (again), and Marvel doesn't seem to have enjoyed it much. She seems tired and distracted. I try to get her to hang out awhile, but eventually bring her back to the apartment building.

Later that night, she sends me an e-mail.

Thanks for tonight. Even though I didn't really like the movie, it made me think. I keep a journal—did I tell you that? I wrote this and thought I'd share.

I open the attached document. I'm surprised she had the time to write it, and even more surprised she had the guts to send it to me.

SUPERMAN

What would we say if he came down now? Today? This
*   very moment?*
What hope would he offer? What promise would he give?
How would he stand out in our world full of sounds and
*   images and atrocities and wonders?*
How would he get our attention?
How would he speak the truth and let the glory and the
*   majesty rush over us like the waves of Niagara Falls?*

How would we know he was the one and only true son?
How could we see in a world that lets us see everything and
feel everything and be anything?
How would we know? And why would we care?
What brokenness inside us could be repaired?
What yearnings could finally be satisfied?
What noise could finally be stilled?
How would we know our one and only superhero if we
saw him today, in the flesh?
And seeing him, and realizing his true identity, how could
we accept it? How? How?
A Superman awaits. And not even Kryptonite will stop him.

I gotta admit, I have goose bumps after reading this. I know it's because Marvel wrote it and because I can still hear the movie's theme song in my head. But maybe it's because of something else. I don't know.

I text her back, **That was beautiful. You should put that online.**

Thank you. Like where? she replies a moment later.

I think of the time Devon had a blog called "All the Things in Appleton That Smell Bad." It was short-lived but funny.

You should do a blog.

Maybe. Thanks for reading it.

Thanks for sharing it.

Good night!

I look back over her article, and a couple of lines stand out.

What brokenness inside us could be repaired?
What yearnings could finally be satisfied?

Good questions, Marvel. I'm just not so sure your Superman really does await. 'Cause I've been waiting a long time and still don't see any sign of him.

Maybe I'm wrong, though. Maybe the signs have started popping up everywhere.

54

"No."

It's the one word I can't hear my mom tell me.

"It's just for one day," I say to her. Again.

Mom is cleaning up after dinner, and I was hoping to ask her at a busy time. She acts like she's already had a conversation with Dad.

"Your father isn't going to let you go to an expensive concert. Even if the ticket was given to you."

"I already told them I was going," I say.

"You'll have to tell them you're not going anymore."

"Mom, seriously—"

"Talk to your father then."

Whenever Mom says this, I know I'm done. There's no way I'm going to talk to Dad about Lollapalooza.

"Mom, can you just talk to him?"

She hands me the ketchup and mustard. "Put this away while you're here."

We had hamburgers and hot dogs on the grill. Grilling is

just another excuse for Dad to drink. Like a sporting event. Or a holiday. Or breathing.

Carter comes in and asks what I'm wanting. "Nothing," I tell him.

"He wants to go to a concert in Chicago," says Mom. "Where were you during dinner?"

"I was playing basketball at the Grambs'."

Carter can get away with things because he's athletic and Dad loves him. Sometimes it drives me crazy, because I think he's always playing the jock card.

"What concert?" he asks, going to the fridge and getting out the burgers we just put into a container. "Hey, where's the ketchup?"

I want to pour the ketchup over his head. "Here you go." I toss it, and of course he catches it without even thinking about it.

"I bet if there was some kind of sporting event, Carter'd be able to go," I say to Mom.

She ignores me, but Carter takes a bit of a cold hamburger and nods. "Yeah, probably."

There might be a time when he's going to need me for something, and if and when he does, well, I just might not be around.

Yeah, right.

"Mom, just this one time, please, that's all I ask."

But Mom doesn't want to hear it. She's moved on. The only thing I can do is try to do the same.

A couple of days later I'm still debating whether to completely disobey my mother or just try to sell the ticket and give Harry his money back. I'm sure Marvel will understand. I'm also sure she'll still want me to go to church with her.

I'm driving Glyn's truck far more often this summer than I thought I would be. It's rattling and I'm hoping it doesn't break down with me in the driver's seat.

I head down the busy street toward the water tower. I've passed it a thousand times before. It says Appleton in big letters, and underneath: *A Small Place with Big Potential.* The guys and I joke about that phrase a lot. But as I drive toward it, suddenly the saying doesn't seem funny.

Suddenly the water tower is blank.

Since the sun is bright I blink several times to determine whether what I'm seeing is real. That's when the words change.

DON'T STOP

I blink and hold my eyes closed, then look again.

JUST GO

When I see these two words, I almost crash the truck I'm driving. I steady it and drive past the water tower at forty miles an hour. In the mirror I look for writing anywhere else, but I don't see anything. I'm not about to slow down.

I just made that up. That didn't just happen.

But I can blink and still see those words.

Don't stop.

Just go.

Really? Am I seriously losing it or something?

55

I'm at a Kane County Cougars game with Devon and his family when I get a text.

Just completely lost it. Bawling like a baby. Wish I could see you.

Some things in life don't need second-guessing.

Devon had driven us to the minor league baseball field, and his parents had come separately. I turn to him and say, "Hey, can I borrow your Jeep?"

For a second he gives me an odd look. Devon knows I wouldn't ask to borrow his new Jeep without a serious reason. I show him Marvel's text.

"She just sent this?"

I nod.

"Okay then." He hands me the keys. "I can ride home with my parents. Just let me know when you'll bring it back."

"I seriously owe you, man."

Devon explains that I have a family emergency, and I thank his parents and take off. As I'm walking toward the parking lot, I text Marvel back.

Where can I meet you? Tonight I have a car.

I'm in the library.

So what kind of book are you reading? I ask, trying to be funny.

I'll be waiting outside.

I take her to this little burger and ice cream joint that's only open in warm weather. We both get ice cream cones, though it seems like neither of us is very hungry. We sit at a table next to an older couple working on some kind of sundae and another table with a family all eating cones.

"So what's up?"

"Everything," Marvel says.

I nod, not sure what *everything* refers to and hoping I'm not a part of it.

"I was reading an article about Artie. I've stayed away from watching the news about it, but I came across a newspaper giving details. It's awful."

"Yeah."

"I'm scared. I'm scared that things are only going to get worse."

"Why? We're probably safer now than we've ever been before. I swear I've lost track how many times during the day I see random cop cars patrolling, waiting for anything weird."

"I just think of the next year and it's overwhelming," she says, sounding weak and defeated.

"Look, I'll help you out in any way I can at school."

"I know—thank you. It's not that."

"It's just a little bit of everything, huh?"

"The book of Revelation—which I don't understand at all, to be honest—says that in heaven there will be no night and no need for lamps or sun because the Lord will shine on us. I love thinking about that. I love thinking that the darkness won't have a place anymore. The darkness outside and the darkness in our hearts."

I keep eating my ice cream cone. How can I respond to something like that?

"I know you think I'm crazy," Marvel says.

"No, I don't. Honestly."

"A little crazy then."

"Yeah, sure. But so am I."

"Thank you, Brandon. Thanks for being so kind to me this summer."

I nod. "You're different from the girls around here."

"I'm different from most people. Always have been."

"Different is good," I say.

"Sometimes."

"I can't wait to go to Lollapalooza. The weather looks like it's going to be nice."

"I'll try to be in better spirits."

"I like the fact that you can be honest about being sad. I think . . . I think I've gone a long time not thinking about my feelings. Maybe thinking I shouldn't even have them. I'm the oldest of three guys, and one thing my father has tried to get me to believe is that I just gotta suck it up. Be a man and take the hits and blah blah blah."

"Blah blah blah," Marvel says with a smile.

"Yeah, and I think I've gotten used to sorta believing it and not being emotional and all that. But then I meet you."

"A real basket case."

"Are you kidding? You have it all together, considering everything."

"I hide it well," Marvel says.

"I think we all do. I think everybody has secrets. Every family. Some are worse—or more weird—than others. But we all have them. And it's cool to meet someone who is a little more up front about them."

Marvel smiles, but she seems sad again.

"Hey—okay, now what'd I say?" I ask.

"Nothing. Nothing. You're precious, you know that?"

"That makes me sound like a kitten."

"Kittens are special."

"Please," I say. "I'll be anything other than a kitten."

She smiles, and everything inside of me wants to lean over the table and kiss those smiling lips. But I'm precious, and precious people don't do that sort of thing, right?

It doesn't matter what I am. It matters that I can sit here with her and make her smile and try not to think of the overwhelming next year. Whatever it brings, I want Marvel to know I'll be around.

56

On the way home from Devon's house, close to eleven o'clock, I see a figure standing in someone's lawn across the street underneath some trees. For a second, I wonder if it's my father. But Dad wouldn't be hiding. If he came out here to find me, he'd find me. He wouldn't worry about hiding in the shadows.

I stop for a moment and look. If it's some weirdo, he'll go away. But this person just stands there. It's clear that I'm looking at him, not moving in any way.

I keep walking down the sidewalk, and the figure across the street moves too, keeping pace with me.

"Hey—you need something over there?" I call.

I think of all the times Mom has told us to be careful, all the cop warnings, all the adults telling us not to be out alone at night. I can hear Harry saying, "What are you doing, you idiot?" But after being around Marvel all night, I'm feeling high and a bit cocky.

The figure stands there. He's wearing a sweatshirt with the hood up. Half of me wants to walk over and see who it is.

"Can I help you?" I say.

The shadow just stays there, waiting, watching. It's seriously creepy. Was this what happened to Artie? Was he followed slowly, then lost track of the figure until it was upon him and started cutting him all over?

Stop that now, Brandon.

I keep walking, constantly looking over to make sure he's there. To make sure he's not suddenly sprinting toward me with a meat cleaver in his hand. My house is only six houses away. The figure moves with me until we hear a car approaching. Then I see an SUV passing, and the creeper suddenly disappears.

I make it to the house safely. For now.

He might have just been trying to scare me, whoever this weirdo is. But he doesn't have a clue that the thing I'm most scared of resides behind the door I quietly open.

Thankfully, it appears I'm safe for the night.

I see a car driving at eighty miles an hour down a lonely road in the middle of the country. No, it's not the country, it's a suburb west of Appleton. I can't tell if the car is racing toward me or away. Something about this car is not right.

Then I see a helicopter following, and as my view pans away I see multiple cop cars following from all directions. Soon the racing car stops and the driver gets out and runs into a field. Maybe I've seen this before in a movie and that's why I'm dreaming about it now, but it feels very real. It seems like I know who the driver is.

Is that me?

But I don't think it's me. I try to make out the face, and then I see figures dressed like a SWAT team racing out to surround the person. He raises his hands and the figures swarm around him, forcing him to the ground.

More cop cars arrive on the scene. Whatever this guy has done, it's bad. It's really awful.

I keep trying to look at his face to see if it's someone I know, a friend or an enemy or a casual acquaintance. But there is no face to see. Only laughter. Awful laughter. The kind that's loud and awful enough to wake me up.

For a moment I swear I can see blood on my hands. But it's dark and it's three in the morning and I'm imagining things. Bizarre and crazy things that hopefully don't mean anything. That hopefully are just wacky dreams.

57

We sit facing the front of the Metra train. About a third of the people in our train are heading to the same destination. I can tell because of their wristbands and concert wear, and also because about half look seriously wasted. I can't imagine spending a whole weekend at Lollapalooza with a hundred thousand other people. The fortysomething guy who looks like the walking dead maybe should've just imagined it instead of living it.

Marvel takes out her phone. I see she's got headphones attached to it. She's wearing a tank top with yet another flowery dress and matching floral beads around her head. She seriously seems like she could have been teleported from the seventies.

"Gonna just listen to your own music?" I ask.

"It's funny that *you* got me to go to this show, since I like music more than you do."

"I like music."

"Really. Name your top bands."

Nothing really comes to mind. I rattle off a few bands just to name them.

"Come on," Marvel says. "Seriously. Here, I'm going to play you some of my favorites."

"Oh, no. Here we go. Stevie Nicks marathon."

She shakes her head. "No, that's too cliché. I'm going to play you some of my favorites that are out now."

For the next twenty minutes, as we stop at every town on the train line heading east into Chicago, Marvel plays me her special Lollapalooza set list. Some of the music is from bands playing today. Others are just songs she loves. Or, in her words, "beloved songs."

The one thing about all these songs is that they're unique. Like Marvel. They sound like someone I've heard before but they're doing their own thing in a unique way. I make fun of a few of the contemporary songs, but they're all good. As we near the train station downtown, I start to take off the headphones, but Marvel makes me keep them on.

"Listen to the last song."

I fast-forward to get to it.

"That's a special song to me," she says as she takes an earbud out of one of my ears, then sticks it back in.

The song starts slow with a high-pitched female voice singing and a violin playing along. Then I hear the chorus. The word *fear* stands out. I glance at Marvel watching me, watching as someone else sings words that obviously mean something to her.

"I fear I have nothing to give," the singer sings.

It's a hypnotic, trancelike song that fits with the jittery motion of the train and the buildings going past. Marvel watches me, so intense and so *there*. So right there with me in this song. It fades away just as the train heads into the station.

"That was great," I say.

She nods and takes the headphones. She doesn't want to elaborate, and that's okay. Sometimes that's what songs do. Say the words we're too frightened to try to get out.

"Marvel . . . ," I say before the train has stopped and we're moving with the crowd.

"Yeah?"

"Thanks."

I want her to know that I get it. That I appreciate it. That I maybe understand just a little more. Just a little more and that's great. That's really great because I wasn't expecting it.

I'm going to be grounded for a year after this day, not to mention the wrath I'm going to take from the monster at home. But that's okay. Just for this train ride alone, it's worth it.

It happens in the late afternoon, around five thirty or so. Something magical and completely mysterious. Like the girl next to me.

It's a perfect Sunday afternoon, about twenty degrees cooler than usual for this time of year, with a soft breeze coming off the lake. Maybe Chicago knew Marvel was coming and wanted to welcome her. We've watched a few groups, and it's been fun. Everyone's in good spirits and lots of people are stretched out on the grass and dirt of Grant Park. We're checking out this group called Alt-J that's unlike anything I've ever heard. They're funky and groovy (perfect for a seventies vibe) with some amazing percussion and a singer who goes really high and sings strange words.

The clouds have come in. Not storm clouds, but the kind that seem to be hazy like some kind of cool color-altering photo app on your phone. The sun cuts through them as this band plays. Marvel and I are standing as we have before, side by side, like friends would do. But a strange dude dancing to the music causes Marvel to move in front of me. She stays there, since we're surrounded by people.

The band plays a slow song that starts to build. Maybe it's because I've been around her all day, and maybe it's because I'm just embracing the moment. Or maybe it's because it's finally time. I don't know. I just know that I move toward Marvel and slip my arms around her, holding her from behind. She doesn't jerk or elbow me or ask what in the world I'm doing. She stays and even seems to lean back a bit to let me know this is okay.

"A wave, an awesome wave," the guy sings.

And yes, it's an awesome wave.

I see birds flying above, a couple of them seeming to dance together, watching all of us from so high, doing their ballet in the clouds in case we're watching.

I hold this girl I still barely know but want to fully know in every way possible. This girl I went to church with this morning, this girl I know has gone through hell in the past year, this girl who is just like I am, a girl who is just trying to get by.

I hold her and hope it will mean something tomorrow and the next day. I didn't expect to meet her this summer, but her smile walked into the room and has remained in my mind ever since. The wind blows against us and the crowd stirs with electricity and I know that as long as I live, I'll never forget this moment.

I tell Marvel I want to go see Phoenix, but of course she says she wants to see the Cure, that eighties band that Harry loves and I still don't fully get. I'm just wanting more fun moments with Marvel, and I can't see having any during a set list of songs I don't recognize.

"Come on, it'll be great," she says.

And as the sun sets and the band comes on, it really is great. The crowd isn't so packed, and there are a lot of older people singing every song as if they just memorized the lyrics. We move and dance a little and try to sing along.

An hour into the act, they're playing an upbeat song when something happens. Something that makes me think someone slipped something in my Coke earlier. It's nighttime, and the only lights are from the thousands of bulbs penetrating the darkness and shining on the band. Suddenly everything gets bright.

Like really, really bright.

The world around us seems to stop. Not because every-body stops dancing, but because they all just . . .

They all disappear.

Everybody. Every single person.

The bright light is all around, and we're still standing in this field. The music is still playing and the singer is still singing about heaven. I blink and do this thing again with my eyes.

Because this is becoming a little routine, right Brandon?

I blink and open my eyes and see bright light. Then close and open them again and see bright lights.

The sun is brilliant and the sky is blue and Marvel is standing next to me. She reaches out and holds my hand, and then she sways my arm back and forth as if she has no idea this is happening. And it's probably not. I've already seen enough people drinking and smelled enough pot to know there are a lot of people getting high and lit up right this very second. Maybe somehow it's happening to me, too.

But it's not and you know it.

I look out and see the dark blue of Lake Michigan. Then I see Marvel's dark brown eyes and her smile. I smile back and let her know I'm okay. This is a bit crazy but it's okay. She's holding my hand, and I still have no idea if she really *likes* me. But I know she likes me enough to be here with me and be my friend and tell me her deepest, darkest secrets.

The song ends and the applause mounts and then suddenly the lights go out again. It's dark and I'm back in the crowd just like earlier.

They keep playing, and I don't say a word. I'm too freaked out to say anything. Freaked out in a good and a bad way.

We're walking across the field back to the streets and the train when I say to Marvel, barely loud enough for her to hear it, "Did you see that?"

"Did I see what?"

"During the song. The heaven song. Everything just got— everything turned bright."

Marvel stops. "What?"

I stop too. For a second I'm in disbelief. I can't believe she actually knows what I'm talking about.

"Did you see it too?"

"Brandon, don't—please don't . . ."

"Don't what?"

"Don't tease."

"How can I—what am I teasing about? The whole thing— it suddenly became daylight. Everybody was gone. Everybody but you. But the music was still playing and I could hear the singer and—"

Marvel almost tackles me with a hug, squealing a bit like some young girl seeing her favorite boy band live in person.

"Brandon!" she shouts.

"What?"

She sighs and releases me. Then she looks up to the night sky.

"Thank you, God. Thank you."

I wait for an answer to why she's thanking God and why she's so happy, but none comes. I assume it has something to do with the vision/dream/light show I saw, but she doesn't say. She just takes my hand and holds it as we walk back to the train.

Whatever has just happened, I'm not going to mess around with it. At this rate I might even get a good-night kiss.

 **58**

It's after midnight when I get back home. No lights are on inside, and no one is waiting up for me. I slip up the stairs and into my room. I'm not even going to bother brushing my teeth. I'm just going to hit the bed and pass out.

I've been in darkness for about five minutes when the door opens and the light goes on. Mom stands at the doorway, looking tired and angry.

"You disobeyed us," she says.

I don't say anything.

"You're lucky your father is asleep."

I want to tell her, *You're lucky he's not in prison.* But then again, Mom is not lucky. She's made the mistake of being with him.

"We'll talk about this in the morning, but you're grounded from doing anything except working for the rest of the summer."

She turns off the light and shuts the door. It's a good thing, too, since there's a big, fat smile on my face.

"Man, you're in trouble," Alex says to me as I'm getting some cereal.

Mom and Dad are both gone, which is strange since Dad is usually somewhere around.

"Dad flipped out. Mom had to calm him down. Said he was going to have a heart attack."

It's nice that my brother is so concerned about me being in trouble.

"Was it fun?" he asks.

"Yeah."

"Hope it's worth it, since you'll be grounded the rest of your life."

Being in the house makes me nervous, especially since I don't know where Dad is. I get out of there as soon as I can.

I've been at the record store for an hour when Seth walks in. I nod at him, not sure if he's coming in to check out some music or because I work here. I'm dragging today and don't have the energy to try to be nice to someone who's never been nice to me.

He walks up to me. "Hey, man. I got something for you." He hands me a flat paper bag and says, "Go ahead, open it up."

I pull out a comic book in a sealed plastic holder. It's an X-Men comic that looks to be in good condition.

"It's from 1980, and it's in excellent shape. That's issue number 137, the one where Phoenix dies."

I nod, but I have no idea who Phoenix is.

"Do you know X-Men at all?"

"I've seen the movies," I say.

"That's okay. It's a valuable issue. I actually have a couple of them. I wanted to give it to you to thank you. For everything. I haven't really—I didn't want to admit I needed help, but thanks."

"Yeah, man, sure. It was no problem. You didn't have to give me anything. But thanks."

"Sure."

Harry comes in and sees Seth. "How are you doing today?"

Seth gives him a passive, almost blank look. "Fine."

"This a friend of yours?" Harry asks me.

I nod. "Yeah. This is Seth."

Harry shakes his hand. Seth honestly doesn't quite know what to say or do. He seems shocked that I called him my friend. After Harry wanders off, I ask Seth if he's had any more encounters.

"No. I'm lying low."

"Good to hear."

He studies the place but doesn't seem too interested in it. For a moment I think about suggesting that we do something together, but I can't. It just doesn't seem like it would work. Devon and the rest of the guys would never go for it. Seth probably wouldn't either.

I slip the comic back into the paper bag. "Thanks a lot for this."

For a moment Seth seems to be waiting for something else. As if I need to give him something. But I'm not sure what to give him.

"Do you, uh—want to look around?"

Seth shakes his head and looks at me for another moment. "See you around."

"Yeah," I tell him. "See you around."

There's more I probably should say, but I don't really know what. I watch him walk up the stairs in his odd way, then see him head outside.

I'm avoiding going home. I think I seriously might just start living with Devon for the remainder of my teenage years. Frankie and Barton are over, and we've been playing video games. I think so far four thousand people have been shot or beheaded or blown up since we've been hanging out tonight.

"So was Lollapalooza worth it?" Frankie asks.

"Yes."

"How bad did you get in trouble?" Barton asks.

"I'm still waiting to find out."

Barton just laughs and mocks me for a while.

"So are you guys a thing now?" he eventually asks.

"No. We're just friends."

Devon is machine-gunning down a whole squad of zombies. "The thing I don't get with girls is the whole friends thing. They know that we're guys and they know when we're into them, and yet they always just want to be 'friends.'"

"They're waiting for the next great thing," Barton says.

"Marvel is different," I say.

"Yeah, right," Barton shouts. "They're all the same. Just wait till she gets to school. Just wait until the football team starts asking her out."

"You haven't even seen her," I say.

"Yeah, I have. I've gone into the record store."

"When I wasn't there?"

"Yeah. I know what you look like."

We all laugh.

"I'm telling you, this girl is different."

"What if she starts dating Greg Packard?"

I shake my head and deliberately kill a bunch of zombies. "Nope. Not going to happen."

"Girls *love* football players," Barton says.

I could try to tell them otherwise, but I'd just make things worse for myself. I know these guys too well.

"I can't believe school is almost here," Barton says.

"I can't believe football season is almost here," I say, getting an evil look from Frankie.

Devon is the only one still alive at the end of the game. "I can't believe these games are so easy."

I don't want to get off this couch. I want to take these three guys back home with me. But I know I can't. I know I have to step out of the world of zombies and back into the world of reality, where hits cause pain and blood tastes very, very real.

59

Dad is waiting in the driveway with the car running. I curse and stop on the sidewalk, wondering whether to run back inside. But I know if I run away tonight he'll just be there tomorrow. All I can do is keep walking and hope I get a tongue-lashing and nothing more.

The window of the Chevy Malibu is rolled down, and Dad is slumped back. For a second I wonder if he's asleep. Then I see him take a drag from his cigarette.

He's smoking. Not a good sign.

"Get in," he says.

My body tightens and I wonder if this is the moment. When I tell him no more. When I look into that ugly face that somehow kinda resembles me and tell him where he can go and what he can do with himself.

"Get in."

And that's what I do. I don't stand up to him. I move around the car and get inside. I smell the strange mixture of smells on Dad's breath, all bad. I think if hell is real it's going to smell like that awful breath. It's the smell of anger and hate and regret and punishment. I bet it's worse than the smell of death.

He backs the car up and tries to put it into drive, but he's having a hard time. He's completely plastered. I need to get out of the car right now.

"You're gonna learn that when I say somethin' it means somethin', you got that?"

He's slurring like crazy and jerking the gear shaft. I'm tempted to help, but I know he'd just try to break my hand.

When he finally manages to get the car moving, we slowly make it down our street, then turn. His eyelids droop as if he might be going to sleep any minute. I notice he's got a bottle propped between his legs. I study it for a moment and suddenly feel more sick than I've ever felt in my entire life.

That's not a bottle, that's the butt of a gun.

He drives down another street, then takes a turn. This is the way we get to the quarry.

The quarry that's abandoned and in the middle of nowhere and has a steep hill near it. If I don't get shot we might end up toppling the car over.

Dad speeds up and then looks at me and laughs. It seems like he just got a shot of adrenaline or hysteria. Or maybe the demon inside of him woke up.

"You look scared, son," he says. "Scared. Scared."

He keeps repeating the word and gets louder and louder. He's facing me and he looks like the devil and I seriously think about taking the wheel and jerking it to make us crash. But the lights of a vehicle coming out of nowhere behind us do that for me.

There's a loud crash, and the car suddenly veers left toward a tree, and everything turns black.

"Not yet."

My eyes open to see Marvel sitting next to me on the side of a creek. The grass is thick and the sky above us an unending sheet of blue. She puts her hand in mine.

"It's not your time, I know that."

I look at Marvel and see those dark brown eyes. These two worlds of hope staring at me. I try to answer her but can't.

"You're going to be okay. It's all going to be okay. He's in jail for drunk driving. It's amazing you two aren't in worse shape."

I hear her words clearly, but they don't quite match this scene. I look around and see a pack of dogs running together.

Okay, what? Seriously? A pack of dogs?

"I know you can hear me, Brandon. I know somewhere in there you can hear me. So I need to tell you this. I'm not leaving you. Not now and not anytime soon. Do you hear me?"

I want to tell her yes and put my arms around her and hold her and not let her go, but I can't. All I can do is hear her and see her in this strange, beautiful place.

"I've been looking for someone real all my life. I've been running and I've been hurting. And finally, after letting go of all of it, I'm given this gift. A friend I never thought I'd have. I'm given a mirror of sorts, and that mirror is you, Brandon. This guy who smiles and jokes and makes me feel at ease, but carries all this hurt and sorrow around with him. It's hidden away like a field of flowers in a dark cave. It's just waiting to see the sunlight again."

I glance at Marvel and see the flower in her hair.

A flower in her hair? I'm making all this up as the words are being uttered, right?

"You are not alone in that sorrow, Brandon. You are not alone. I'm going to be there for you. And I hope and I pray that one day you'll find your way out of the cave. I pray that you'll finally see God's light waiting for you. I always knew it was there, then it swallowed me whole and saved me."

A bluebird passes by me as I start to leave this magical place.

"There's a safe place you can find down here. I know that. 'Cause I found it, Brandon. And it's an amazing place to be."

The creek and the field behind us and the pack of dogs and the bluebird all fade away. I open my eyes and see Marvel at the edge of my hospital bed. Everything is different except the eyes looking at me.

They are still the same. Still beautiful and still so full of hope.

"Hi," I tell her.

"I've been here for a while," she says.

"I know. I know now."

A day after my father took us joyriding while he had a .32 blood alcohol rate, I leave the hospital. Mom walks me out, and I get in the minivan with her. I have lots of cuts on my face, not to mention a swollen black eye to match the other one my father gave me. Maybe I should be feeling shame or hurt or bewilderment, but honestly, I'm just tired.

"Are you okay?" Mom asks.

"I think I'm going to hurl."

"Really? We can go back in—are you sure? Just hold on—"

"Mom, I'm kidding."

I blacked out when I slammed into the windshield. They monitored my concussion, but I'm lucky. Dad, I think, escaped with barely a scratch. Of course, he escaped straight to jail, where he still happens to be.

"You sure—"

"Mom, I'm fine."

I've seen Mom break down about four times today already,

so maybe I shouldn't be mean to her, but I'm trying to act normal. She grilled me about what happened and why Dad drove off and what in the world he was doing with a gun. I downplayed everything. I just said he wanted to take a drive.

The car that hit us is nowhere to be found. That's a weird thing, something that has everybody from Mom to the cops freaked out. I don't know. I would've believed Marvel was driving it, but she only showed up later.

Turns out Devon heard the crash from his house and was the first one at the scene, and he was the one who called Marvel. The conversation I had with her was early this morning as I was coming out of a weird coma thing.

"You need rest," Mom tells me, speaking above the noise of the whining minivan.

The funny thing is I feel better than I have for a long time. Because I know this: Dad is in jail. He's not home waiting for me to arrive. He's not going to punch me in the ribs or bash a bottle over my head. He's not going to do a thing. So I don't need rest. I think I need to party. Of course, I don't tell Mom this.

Nobody is exactly sure what happened with the other car. But the reality is—and this is what I told the police— somebody came out of nowhere and hit us. Was it Dad's fault (probably) or someone else's? Doesn't matter, because Dad got the blame. And I was able to walk away.

I don't know what's going to happen next. To Dad and to Mom and to our family and to me. My head hurts too much to even think about it. All I want to do is see Marvel again.

62

Later that day, as I'm watching TV in the basement and feeling like I just got run over by a car (hey, wait a minute, I *did*), Devon texts me.

You're not going to believe this.

At this point I'm thinking I'll believe anything.

What? I text.

A girl in St. Charles was just found dead. She was sixteen years old.

What happened?

For a moment I wait as the screen shows Devon furiously typing back.

Cut up with the remains of her body found along river. Remains. They said "remains."

Nothing about this interests me. For a moment I think of my father with the gun in his lap. It's an awful thought.

I think there's a serial killer around here, Devon texts.

I think it's time to move, I text back. And I'm not joking, either. I want to get out of this house and this place. And I want to take Marvel with me.

I see Mom later in the day. So far I haven't spoken that much to Alex and Carter about the accident and about Dad. I don't talk with them about much anyway, so I sure don't want to talk to them about that. It turns out Mom has just been with him.

"He's going to be staying away from the house for a while and getting some help."

I'm not sure I understand what she means. "Some help? For what?"

"For his drinking."

I'd like to ask if he's also getting help for his anger and abuse issues. And maybe also for being a total psycho. But I don't say anything.

"How are you feeling?" she asks me.

"Okay. Did you hear they found someone else in the river?"

Mom shakes her head and tightens her lips. "Anyone you know?"

"No. Some girl from St. Charles."

She lets out a long sigh. "You have to make sure you always—*always*—stay around with your friends. And you watch out for your brothers, Brandon. You hear me?"

Chances are a lot better I won't be hurt now that Dad's gone.

"Yeah."

"I mean it, Brandon. Pay a little more attention to them than you usually do."

"Okay."

"This is an evil world we live in," Mom tells me.

Yeah.

She doesn't need to say it out loud for me to know this.

63

It's late at night, and Frankie, Devon, Barton, and I are all in my basement. The television is low and we're talking about death. All of us seem bummed and a bit freaked out, even the usually full-of-nonsense Barton. I think with the accident last night and the news about the girl today, we all just want to talk out feelings we're not even sure we have.

"What's up with the river?" Barton asks. "He's probably going to be known as the Fox River Killer or something like that."

"I already saw that in the news," Frankie says.

"There are news trucks everywhere," Devon says. "Everybody loves a good story."

"I kinda *want* school to start now," Barton says. "I'm tired of all this boogeyman-in-the-night stuff."

"What if the killer is someone we know?" Devon asks.

I instantly think of my father. I know I have to stop doing this. But how can I not?

"That's a nice thought," Frankie says, tossing a pillow toward Devon.

"I'm telling you. They normally look like ordinary people."

"They normally look like people like you," Barton jokes.

"You feel okay?" Frankie asks me.

"Yeah. Just tired."

"We can leave," he says.

"I'm not going home after all this freaky talk," Barton says.

"Any of you can spend the night," I tell them.

"I can't wait to be interviewed again by some detective about someone I don't even know," Devon says.

"You never did go see a cop about anything, did you?"

He shakes his head. Barton doesn't catch the comment, but Frankie does and asks about it.

Devon says in a very matter-of-fact way, "I've just noticed some strange things happening around our little town."

"The body was found in St. Charles," Barton says. "And just so you know, the river flows *toward* us."

"Thanks. Didn't realize that, Sherlock."

"I hated those movies."

"There are *books* those were based on," Devon says. "Oh, wait, you don't read."

"Not unless it has pictures in it."

I think of the comic book Seth gave me and wonder again what's going to happen with him once school starts. I began the summer not wondering about anything. I was content to just go to work and earn some money and make it through, and then it seemed like everything just changed.

"I think there's been enough drama for twenty-four hours," Devon says. "Don't you think?"

He's looking at me. I just nod and don't say anything.

I get this feeling that this is only the beginning of something really awful. Maybe that's Marvel getting inside of my head, but I can feel it. Well, I can feel the meds I'm taking and they're making me a bit loopy, but I swear I can feel something. Something heavy and weird and not so good.

I hope whatever I feel is dealt with as quickly as possible. I hope it doesn't linger, because this isn't a good feeling. It feels suffocating.

Scary thing is that it also feels like it's just starting.

64

There's no way I could have said no to mowing the Duncans' grass when Harry asked. Artie surely was the one who used to do it, and now a variety of people are helping out. Harry asks me if I can mow it on a weekly basis. I say of course.

I don't knock on the door and don't see anybody around the house. It looks like a normal house just like ours and so many others. But everything about this feels different.

Their son died.

I notice the sidewalk in front of their house. The small walkway leading up to their front door. I bet a lot of people have been through that door this summer. But now it looks almost abandoned.

I know there's got to be a lot of pain inside those doors. Just like the doors to our house.

Just like the doors to a lot of houses.

I'm trying to finish fast when I notice a figure at the window. It's Mrs. Duncan. She's looking out at me, so I wave, but she doesn't wave back. I can see her face clearly. She looks lost and teary.

I don't look that way again for a few moments, feeling awkward and unsure what to do. When I finally look at the window again, it's empty.

All I want to do is finish the job and leave. I have no kind of hope to offer here. No way to help them out in the least. I'm still struggling to make sense of everything myself. I haven't even started to.

I've just finished mowing the Duncans' lawn when I see Marvel rushing across the grass toward me. It's been a few days since I saw her (barely) in the hospital. She looks upset. I'm about to say something when she plows into me like the car that hit us the other night. I almost fall over, but she helps me stay balanced. She wraps her arms around me in the way I've hoped she would all summer long.

"Are you kidding me, Brandon Jeffrey?"

"What? What'd I do? What's wrong?"

I see a car parked on the street. It must be her aunt.

"Nothing is wrong. Everything is right. You are insane, you know that?"

Her hair is pulled back in a ponytail, and she looks like the perfect sort of girl you'd meet on the perfect sort of a summer afternoon. She beams like the sun above us.

"You've been working for *free* all summer? Are you kidding?"

I don't know what to say.

"Brandon, that's crazy. Especially since you have a car to pay off."

"Harry told you."

"*Yes*, Harry told me."

"How?" I ask. "Or why?"

"He felt awful for what happened and told me that if I don't realize the kind of guy you are, I'm crazy."

"He said that?"

"Yeah."

I laugh. "He could've just paid me."

"He plans to. Brandon, what were you thinking?"

"Well, I was hoping—I don't know. I wasn't thinking, really. I just enjoyed being with you. Plus, Harry doesn't pay that much anyway."

She looks at the car and back at me. "My aunt is waiting for me. I had to track you down here."

"How'd you do that?"

"I went by your house. Met—who is your younger brother? Blond and really cute?"

"That'd be Carter. Just don't tell him that. He already has a big head for a twelve-year-old."

"Brandon, why would you do something like that for me?"

I shake my head. "I don't know. I just—it felt like the right thing to do. Even after you said you couldn't and you shouldn't and blah blah blah."

She smiles. "Blah blah blah."

"Yeah."

"I sorta am crazy about this blah blah blah."

"Yeah, me too," I say.

I can tell she's nervous about keeping her aunt waiting.

"Listen, Brandon. It's time, okay. It's just—it's time, but I can't now."

"You want to elope to Vegas?"

She laughs. "No. But I have some things to tell you."

"Uh-oh."

"No. I want to—I need to tell you the truth. Everything."

"Is it going to hurt?"

She wipes more tears away. The sunny, good kind of tears, the sort I kinda like to see.

"Yeah," she says. "It's going to hurt. It's going to hurt to tell you, but you'll understand why. Finally. You will think I'm crazy, but that's okay because you're sorta crazy too."

"Yeah."

"So—just—I'll text you later. Maybe we can—I don't know. Later today. Or tomorrow."

"Okay," I say.

Those almond-shaped eyes give me a hopeful, happy, knowing look. There's so much behind it.

"Brandon, I just . . ."

"Blah blah blah," I finish. "Your aunt is waiting. Call me later. When I'm not so sweaty and smelly."

"Okay."

The girl with the yellow shirt and those bright brown eyes is my summer girl. She tells me good-bye and takes off.

I don't wonder about what she's going to tell me. Whatever it is, I'll listen and try to understand. What I wonder is how I'll move into fall with the summer girl. How school and the changing season will change things with us. For better or for worse.

Marvel looks back at me before she goes.

I have to believe it'll be for the better. I choose to believe it's for the better.

With school coming up and my schedule about to get really busy, I decide to tell Harry I can't work at the record store anymore. Not that I've really been working here the last couple of months. And not that I've really gotten paid, either. It's time, as much as I love being here.

But when I come in I see only Phil, sitting on his stool behind the counter like he always does, listening to Led Zeppelin.

"School starting soon?" he asks me in his slow, cool vibe.

"Yeah."

"Staying out of trouble this summer?"

"Yeah," I say.

He looks at me and one eye squints. "Doesn't look like it."

"It's been a weird summer."

"Yeah." The music keeps cranking on the six speakers that surround us. "Hear about the girl they just found in the river?"

"Yeah."

"That's weird, huh?"

He's got a thick beard and sometimes I think it actually muffles his voice.

"You still hanging around with Marvel?" he asks.

"Yeah."

"Good choice. She's a keeper if you ask me. I'd stay with her."

Just then, Harry rushes out of the back room and sees me. It's kinda funny, the way he's always rushing and running around, yet this place stays dead half the time.

"Brandon," he shouts. "You working today?"

"No, I just came to talk to you about that."

"Cool."

Robert Plant is wailing as if he's in pain. I've gotten used to it, but sometimes it still sounds kinda crazy.

"Marvel's not here, you know," Harry says.

"Yeah, I just wanted to talk about my schedule with school coming up."

Harry holds up a hand as if to stop me from saying more. "Listen, just—hold on a minute, okay? I got something to show you."

This is already hard enough, telling him I won't be working this fall. Not that he really needs me, but I think Harry likes having me around. He takes me out the side door. There's a red SUV parked in the spot Harry usually takes.

"So, I've been thinking long and hard about this. Feeling bad about the whole Marvel thing this summer."

"I know you told her," I say.

"I had to. She needed to know."

"It's okay."

Harry stands next to the car, a Honda Pilot. "Okay, so here's the thing. You still need a vehicle, right? And I want to pay you for your work this summer, even though it's been a bad summer."

"It's fine, Harry."

"Could you see yourself driving this sucker?"

I look at the SUV. "What? That?"

He smiles and nods. "Yep."

"You're gonna give it to me?"

"No. *But.* What if you gave me a hundred bucks for it?"

I laugh. "What? Does it not have an engine or something?"

"No. I got it for a steal. Long story involving my cousin and helping him out. It's almost ten years old and has 150,000 miles on it. But—it's a good vehicle. Has a third row for all your friends."

"For a hundred bucks?"

Harry nods.

"Why?"

"Consider it payment for working here. And for bringing Marvel here. Or I guess I should say for hiring her. She's pretty remarkable."

"Yeah."

I'm not sure what to say. I obviously can't quit now, now that he's basically giving me this Honda.

"I don't know. . . ."

"Listen, Brandon." He glances around, then looks back at me. "I've got three boys. They're young, but I only hope and pray they turn out to be like you. You've got a head on your shoulders. And I know—there's been a lot of stuff going on this summer. When I heard about the accident I just, I got afraid. Afraid something might've happened to you and wondering if I could've done more."

I nod and look away because I know the direction he's heading.

"And, hey, listen. It's not my business, but then again, it's totally my business. The stuff going on around here is crazy and I just—I want to look out for you. This—I was able to help my cousin out and I'm also able to help you and your family out. I'm assuming you're down a car for a while, right?"

"Yeah. Dad's car got pretty trashed."

Just like Dad.

"This is our family helping out. No big deal. No strings attached and no weird feelings accompanying it. Okay?"

Yeah, no way I'm quitting today.

"Thanks."

"Give me a few days to get the title, and I'll sign it over to you when you pay me. And maybe—who knows? Maybe you can take Marvel out in it next weekend."

I laugh. Harry the matchmaker.

"Man, that's really cool," I tell him.

"That's me," Harry says. "Really cool. Next time you see Sarah, you remind her, okay?"

"Promise."

So it looks like I've got a car for my senior year. And it's a step up from the Nissan Barton is still paying me for.

Hopefully this car won't end up crashed. But considering my life, the odds don't look so great.

66

It's been raining all day Thursday. I've spoken with Marvel on and off, and I can tell she's been waiting on seeing me. It's about eight o'clock when I get a text from her.

Can you come to the store? she asks.

When?

Now?

I'm just watching television with my brothers. **Yes.**

I don't have the Honda Pilot from Harry yet, so I'm forced to ride my bike. But I don't care. She wants to see me and is ready to talk, so fine. I've been ready for the last two months.

When I arrive at Fascination Street Records, I'm soaked. Marvel has the door open and is waiting for me with a towel.

"Where'd you find that?" I ask her.

"In the back."

I glance around the store as I'm drying off and brushing back my hair.

"You alone?"

"Harry had to go home. I figured—with the rain and being by myself—it'd be a good time to talk."

She's right. Nobody's going to come in. Not while it's coming down like this.

She looks anxious. "Are you okay?" I ask.

"No," she says quickly. "But that's okay. I just need to get this off my chest and I'll be better. Well, maybe or maybe not."

"Let's get away from the front, okay? In case someone does come."

We move toward the back of the record store where we sell T-shirts and there are a couple of comfortable chairs.

"Are you sure you want to do this?" I ask, sitting down across from her. "I don't want to force you to do anything."

"I've never told anybody the story. Not all of it. I've told people I blacked out when my family got killed. But I didn't. I know everything that happened, Brandon. Everything."

She's shaking. I reach over to touch her, but she jerks away. Then she shakes her head.

"No, just—just let me tell you. Let me tell you before I don't tell you because I don't want to and I might not."

"Okay."

The rain keeps coming down outside, as if it's brought reinforcements and wants to drown out Marvel's voice. For a second the power flickers off, then comes back on. I see the shadowy outline of her face, those eyes glassy but determined.

"I heard my father downstairs when he came in. My mom screamed, and I heard the sound of him hitting her. But this time something was different. I heard some kind of commotion—it was my mother fighting back. She had pulled a knife on him and stabbed him in the arm. That was when he went crazy."

I think I'm shaking now, listening. A part of me doesn't want to hear this story, not the full story. A part of me hovers over myself as if I'm watching the two of us talking.

Just pretend like you're listening but don't fully listen because you don't want to hear what she has to say don't do it Brandon don't.

But of course I have to. I want to know. I want to know how I can help. If I can ever help.

"He took the knife and stabbed her multiple times. I can still hear those sounds, a blunt sound over and over again, a sound that makes me sick. That was when I went into my closet and shut the door. Of course there was no way to hide, not really. Little did I know it wasn't my father I needed to be frightened of anymore. It was what he was about to do."

Suddenly Marvel starts to cry, holding her face in her hands and letting everything spill out. I can't help moving over to her and putting my hand on her arm.

"Marvel—it's okay—you don't have to keep telling me."

"I didn't know my little sister Mirage was in the house. I thought she was at a friend's. But after I smelled the gas I heard her scream. I tried to get out of the closet, but I couldn't. For some reason—well, I know why now—I couldn't open the door. I tried and tried, and she kept screaming and then everything just blew up around me. The entire place went up in flames. I was on the second floor and I couldn't get out."

She shakes, her eyes puffy and red, the tears still streaming down.

"I was coughing and couldn't breathe, and I knew I was going to die just like my mother and probably my sister. I cried out and pounded on the door but it wasn't enough. Until suddenly, everything changed. Every single thing changed, Brandon. And the only way to describe it to you—the only way to sum it up—is to compare it to what happened at Lollapalooza in the middle of the show. When everything changed."

Marvel takes in a nervous breath, swallows, then keeps talking.

"I suddenly could open the door, and all I saw were flames around me. Surrounding me. They were hot and full of black smoke but I wasn't being burned, and I wasn't coughing any-more. I watched from the closet but I was protected. I was safe. Not a single hair on my head was singed."

She wipes her eyes and her cheeks, then looks at me with that intense stare I've seen so many times. The one that always seemed to hold secrets and carry weight. Now I know why. Now I really know why.

"In this closet, as my house burned down all around me, and as the only family I knew were being burned with it, I heard God talk to me. The same way God talked to Moses through the burning bush. Except in this case, the bush was my house. In this case, it was my *life*."

I don't dare speak. I believe every word she says. It doesn't make sense, but it doesn't have to, not now. Right now I'm simply listening. Processing will come later. My skin feels like it's buzzing.

"The voice was something I'd never heard in my life. It was both something I feared and something I loved. It was the voice of a father talking to his daughter the way a father should talk. Warning her, but in a loving way. Commanding her. Telling her why she was being rescued. Telling her the reason.

"In that moment, God said this to me. He told me I would be used for his power and his glory. That I would be used in an awe-inspiring way. I remember him speaking my name, Brandon. I know how it sounds—I mean, I can only imagine. But God spoke and he said my name, and I began to cry because I'd been waiting for that voice to talk to me my whole life. I'd been waiting for this moment and it was terrifying and it was awful, but I knew I was okay. I knew I was loved. I knew I was protected."

Marvel smiles and wipes the tears off her face. She sees my expression and reaches over to grab my hand. To comfort me.

"God told me I was going to go somewhere and I was going to do something special. He said I would be his instrument. He said I shouldn't be afraid, but that I would be used in an incredible way. He said I'd save others from something."

For a second she pauses and looks at me, wanting me to hear exactly what she's saying.

"And then he said I would die being used in this way."

She doesn't give me a chance to respond.

"Then I found myself on the street beside our burning building, protected but coughing and black with the smoke I'd been inhaling. I don't know how I got out of there, but I got out. I mean, I know who got me out. But how, I'm not sure.

"And I know—I know, before all the questions or comments or whatever you might have—there was one final thing God told me. He said he would find a helper for me. That eventually, someone would come to help me. That was it. And Brandon—I really believe that person is you."

"Me?"

I'm a bit shocked to hear how I fit into this story.

"I believe you're the one."

I always had hoped Marvel might say those words. But now they have a far different meaning.

I swallow. "I want to do whatever I can."

"I know this sounds crazy."

I nod. "Yes, it does."

"Do you believe me?"

I keep nodding. "Yeah. I'm trying to."

"The question isn't whether it will happen, Brandon. The question is when. And how."

"I'm sorry," I tell her.

"What? You don't understand?"

"No, I'm sorry—I'm so, so sorry, Marvel. For what you had to go through. For everything."

"Thank you."

The tears start to flow again.

"I'm sorry and I just want you to know I'm here," I tell her. "Okay? For whatever. To help or to hurt someone or to just hang out with you."

"Very brave of you."

"I hate people picking on others."

She smiles. "My Father is bigger than any other father who might come our way. My God is bigger than any of this. I saw it firsthand. I felt it. I heard *Him*. In the middle of a dark hell I saw amazing light and heard an incredible sound. I'm not scared. Well, I am a bit, but not the way I should be."

"I just want to be at your side. For whatever happens. For whatever you need."

"Thank you," Marvel says. "Thank you for not interrupting and not treating me like a crazy person."

"Tomorrow might be a different story," I joke.

"Then I'll stay away for a day or two."

"Don't stay away. For anything."

I hold her and hear the continued storm outside raging. We hug each other for a moment, then Marvel moves and faces me.

"I hope you're ready," she says.

"Ready for what?"

She glances out the window and hears the crackle of lightning. "For anything."

I stare at that face and know I'm ready for anything. For a crazy girl making up a story or for a fortunate girl figuring out her life. It doesn't matter, because I'm here for her. I'm here and plan on being here as long as she'll let me be here.

As long as Marvel wants me to be here. And yes, maybe, possibly, even God, too.

There's more that I want to say, that I need to say, that I need to do, that I want to do, but suddenly the door opens and we see a completely wet Harry come in.

Marvel smiles and wipes her eyes.

I look at her and whisper, "To be continued."

67

I'm riding my bike home in the dark and the rain, and all
I can think about are Marvel's words. Her story. The whole,
complete story. I picture her hiding in her closet, the mad-
man below lighting himself and the rest of the family on fire.
I see her protected and talked to by God. It's crazy, I know it's
totally crazy. Maybe she made up the whole thing in her mind
to block out the pain of what happened with her mother and
sister, but I don't know.

I don't know.

I think of all the years I've blocked out what's gone on
with my father, the hurt and awful pain he's brought me
night after night. The fear of doing something wrong or
slipping up and being completely terrorized. I think of how
many years I've lived in this hell without anybody to tell or
any kind of hope.

Then Marvel walked through the door.

The rain comes down hard, but I don't care. I have a nag-
ging feeling that has nothing to do with bullies or bad guys

or dead bodies or crashed cars or awful things we can't talk about.

I shouldn't be going home. I need to go back to the store and tell Marvel how I'm feeling. I don't want to wait another night. Because tomorrow might not be there.

There might be some stalker up ahead waiting to jump out at me and finally do what he's been wanting to do for a long time. I might end up in the Fox River without any leads or motives or anything for the cops.

I don't want to go to bed without telling Marvel what I need to tell her. I can't wait. I need to tell her, and I need to tell her face-to-face.

I turn the bike around and start pedaling as if my very life depended on it.

By the time I get back to the store, she's waiting in front of the building under the little awning by the Fascination Street sign. Her ride must be coming soon. I'm a sopping mess, but I don't care. I get off my bike and lean it against the side of the building. Lightning lights up the sky, followed by a blast of thunder.

"Brandon!" she says in surprise.

"I needed to come back. To tell you something."

The rain falls, and the door is closed and probably locked. Marvel stands there by the building with wet hair and sad eyes.

"Just hear me out," I say.

I face her and take her hands. For a moment, she hesitates. "No."

"I don't care what happens," I tell her. "I don't care what's meant to happen or what your destiny is supposed to be. I'm crazy about you, Marvel."

"You don't understand. . . ."

"And neither do you. Do you? You believe this . . . this *thing*, but you don't know when it will happen and you don't know what it will be. So let me stand by you. Let me help you. Marvel—let me *love* you."

She shakes her head, tries pulling away, yet I still hold those hands. "Brandon . . ."

"No. I knew. I knew the moment you walked through those doors. I've known ever since all the crazy, weird stuff has been happening. I knew the moment you held my hand and we saw those fireworks going off. Don't tell me it's not there. I know you feel the same. I know it."

"But it doesn't—it shouldn't matter. . . ."

I move closer and hold her in my arms. "But it does matter."

I lean down and kiss her. It feels right, and it definitely matters. Marvel doesn't pull away. She gives me a gentle, affirming kiss that is worth every single moment of waiting this whole summer.

When I step back to look at her, I can't tell whether she's crying. But she has regret and fear on her face. Thunder roars above us.

"The sky can fall and I'm going to stand next to you, Marvel."

She shakes her head. "I didn't want this to happen. I told myself over and over it couldn't happen. That there shouldn't be an *us*. That *we* shouldn't be."

"It happened. Okay? I'm here."

I take hold of her hand again and bring her closer to me. We kiss again.

The storm continues to rage above us, but we're standing here together. The sky might truly fall, but we have found each other.

68

Mom bought pizza, and she made it a point to have all of us sitting around the table. We're wolfing it down when she tells us what's up.

"Your father is coming home tomorrow," she says.

Suddenly I'm not in the mood to eat. Both of my brothers basically look the same way.

"I want us all to make him feel like nothing has happened," Mom says. "He's had a rough time since losing his job, and he's working through a lot of things."

Something inside makes me want to cough up this piece of pepperoni pizza. Maybe it's Mom telling me to act like "nothing happened." Besides, of course, my almost dying in a car accident because Dad was drunk. Maybe it's Mom saying Dad's had a "rough time" and that he's "working through a lot of things." I'd love to tell her the truth about rough times and working through things.

"Is he here to stay?" Alex asks.

"Yes, he's here to stay."

"Where'd he go anyway?" Carter asks.

"A place you go to when you drink all day long," Alex tells him.

"A place to get better," Mom says.

A place that's a Band-Aid on a big, gaping wound that's never going to heal.

"Brandon, are you okay with your father coming home?"

I nod. I'm tired more than anything. Tired of acting, tired of hiding. I'd love to say how I really feel. But I don't. I just nod and eat some more pizza.

"Things are going to get better," Mom says. "Once your father finds where he needs to be, things will be better."

I wonder how a woman more than twice as old as I am can be so utterly clueless. But then again, I'm kind of clueless too. In other ways. In lots of other ways. And I'm glad Mom is clueless. Just because.

"Two kids have died this summer, and it makes me realize life is short. We need to accept each other for who we are. Your father—he's going to change. He's promised me that." Mom looks at me. "Things are going to get better," she says.

Yeah. Okay. I smile and nod and act like I believe her. But I don't and I never will.

I'm midway through cutting a lawn at a house west of the Fox River when I see a cop car drive past and slow down. He stops in front of the house, and I see a hand gesturing me toward him. I wonder if I'm in trouble, even though I haven't done a thing. That's just the feeling I get whenever I see a cop car.

"You're Brandon Jeffrey, right?"

I nod, suddenly worried that something happened to Mom or one of my brothers.

"Everything's fine, don't worry," the cop says.

When I get up close I recognize the man. It's Sergeant Harden. He's got short, blond hair and a square face, and looks like he could've been in the military or a frat house, or both. He's no-nonsense, but he seems friendly. And something in the way he said "Don't worry" makes me do exactly that.

"Had a crazy midnight drive the other night, didn't you?" he asks.

I nod.

"I'm Mike Harden. I know your parents a bit. Listen— you've got friends around here, okay? You need anything, you let me know. Okay?"

"Okay," I say with a hoarse voice.

He glances at me as if waiting on me to say something. But nothing comes. He looks at the lawn.

"Maybe I should get you to cut my lawn, though it's the end of the summer."

"I'm always looking for new business," I tell him.

"Yeah. Good for you. Look, Brandon. You know two dead kids showed up in the river this summer, right?"

"Yeah."

A bit hard not to know.

"You be on the lookout, okay? And do me a favor. Keep an eye on your buddy Devon. He's a bit too curious for his own good."

"Yeah, I know," I say.

I wonder if Devon finally went and talked to him, but I'm guessing he didn't. I'm guessing he's still a bit scared because of the pot he bought from Artie. I probably would be too.

"Do you guys know anything more about what happened?" I ask.

Mike gives me a hard look. "I know this world can be mean and dangerous. I just—I'm thankful for my family. And I worry about them. I worry about kids like you."

I guess even if he did know something, he couldn't tell me.

"Take care of yourself, Brandon."

"Okay."

He drives off, leaving me standing alone on the lawn. I look around and wonder if someone is watching me. I wonder if someone knows where I am at any given point of the day. I wonder if they watch from behind trees and curtains and tinted windows.

I glance around at the neighboring houses. Suddenly I feel afraid, more afraid than I have all summer long. But this time it's not for me. I'm not thinking about who's going to jump out of the dark or who's watching me.

I'm worried for Marvel. I'm worried that I'm not near her, watching over her.

If there's anything I can do—anything I can try to do— I'm going to do it. Maybe she's crazy, maybe this is all in her mind. But if it's not, I want to help. I want to do more than help. A lot more than help.

I want to change whatever she's supposed to do. I want to be there to save her. I don't know how and when and where. I don't know what any of it means. But I'm going to know.

Given enough time, I'm going to find out if she really did hear from God. And if it was God she heard from, I'm going to ask her to tell him to talk to me.

'Cause I have some questions for him. Lots and lots of questions.

I see him from my bedroom window. I've been up here waiting to hear the sound of a car and watching to see the opening door. Dad looks the same. He's shaved and his hair is
combed back and his eyes don't look demonic, but he's the
same. Mom climbs out of the driver's side, since Dad won't be
driving for a while. They walk toward the front of the house,
disappearing from view.

My heart beats fast enough to win a Kentucky Derby.
I want to throw up. I want to climb out of this window and
take off. I want to do anything but go downstairs and see
him. I don't want to tell him hello and I don't want to start
the whole act again.

My skin feels like poison ivy that needs to be scratched
and scratched until it's bloody and raw and open.

I think of Marvel's confession to me and what she said
about hearing God.

*But God spoke and he said my name, and I began to cry
because I'd been waiting for that voice to talk to me my whole*

life. I'd been waiting for this moment and it was terrifying and it was awful, but I knew I was okay. I knew I was loved. I knew I was protected.

My body shivers. I want to cry, but I honestly don't think I can. All I know is that I've been waiting for so long. I've been waiting, but nothing is different. I'm *not* okay. I'm *not* loved.

And God isn't going to protect me from that monster who just walked back through the door of our house. Maybe he'll make everybody think he's changed but on some dark night will lash out again. And when he does, maybe I'll finally have the guts to do what I need to do. Maybe I will show him I'm okay, that I don't need love, that I can protect myself.

Maybe I will bash his ugly face in and show him and God that I don't need them and I can do this thing on my own.

Yeah, maybe. Maybe.

I swallow and taste a bitter sort of taste, the kind you have right before hurling. Then I hear my name called. I shut my eyes. I don't want to do this. I really don't.

I just want to be away from all of this.

71

It's probably the last time the guys and I will hang out at the quarry this summer. The August afternoon is hot, and I'm sitting in the shade watching Frankie and Devon and Barton behaving like idiots in the water. I look at all the people in this swimming hole—the mothers with their little babies and toddlers, the middle school kids just starting to figure themselves out, the couples suntanning for each other. Everybody is acting like it's just another ordinary day, and it sure feels like it. But part of me wonders if something really, truly has been set in motion. Something awful that can't be stopped. Or something that can only be stopped by something Marvel is supposed to do.

"Come on in the water," Frankie shouts to me.

I wave at him, but I don't feel like it. I'm thinking of all these unanswered strands and wondering what will happen with them.

I think of what happened with Marvel's father, what he did to their family. She got out only to go live with an uncle who gives her creepy looks and an aunt who doesn't trust her.

I wonder what it's going to be like when Marvel arrives at school. Who will welcome her (the guys probably) and who won't (Taryn and her friends).

I think of my ex and dread seeing her and her friends again. It's been nice to be away, to have a break from all that nonsense. But soon it'll be back in force. I'll have to deal with Taryn coming up to me day after day with drama after drama.

I think of Seth and wonder how he's going to make it through next year. Will the guys get bored with bullying? Normally, guys are too stupid to get bored with doing something bad. I think it's going to continue. And I think I'm going to keep figuring out ways I can help. Whatever that means.

I wonder when we'll find out more details about the girl from St. Charles who showed up dead in the river. Is her death connected to Artie Duncan's? Is there a serial killer on the loose?

Maybe that's why I suddenly feel so awful, so worried. I'm watching my friends laughing and enjoying themselves, and I wonder what would happen if one of them showed up dead. We all knew Artie, but he wasn't a close friend. But what if? What if?

I close my eyes for a moment and picture my father. I can still see his smile when I greeted him in our house. He acted nice and polite and friendly, but we both know it's just an act. I don't care if he's gotten some help. He's not going to change. I could still see it in his eyes, the fire burning. Like a wick always on, always ready to engulf you in flames.

"Get in here," Frankie calls out again.

Enough worrying and soul-searching and wondering. I can't do anything about those things now. All I can do is dive into the water and keep living life. And that's what I'm going to do.

72

"Hi."

Marvel's voice on the line is always a pleasant surprise.

"What's up?" I ask her.

I'm driving home from cutting a lawn. I was going to see if she wanted to hang out later, whatever that might mean.

"I'm leaving to spend a week in Michigan before school starts."

"Really? Where?"

"The Grand Rapids area. We have relatives there. My aunt's taking some time off work."

"So when do you leave?" I ask.

"In about an hour."

I laugh. "Wow. That's sudden."

"I know."

"So when do you get back?"

"Sunday."

"So I won't even see you before school starts then, huh?"

"I know." She sounds sad. "I was hoping just to see you one more time."

"Yeah."

"Can I see you now?"

I'm a sweaty, grassy mess, but that's okay. "Well, yeah, sure. Why? Are you okay?"

"Yes. I just have something to give you."

"That makes me nervous. Like you're going to give me some kind of special amulet to battle the walking dead."

"Where do you come up with this stuff?"

"I love zombies," I say, half joking.

"It's nothing like that. It's just—it's the equivalent of seeing you one more time before school. It's something I want you to start school with."

"A Lynyrd Skynyrd T-shirt?"

She laughs. This is record store humor, since we always joke about all the Lynyrd Skynyrd shirts we are constantly selling.

"No, no, it's not *that* special," Marvel says.

"I was driving home. I could swing by your apartment."

"I can't leave. But I can at least meet you in the parking lot."

"How romantic."

Marvel is wearing cutoff jeans and a T-shirt that says *Love Peace Joy.* She walks over to my car slowly in her flip-flops. Her hair looks like it's in braids.

"I have to work on looking different every time I see you," I tell her. "Just to compete with you."

"I was bored and my aunt braided my hair."

"I like it."

I'm standing by the side of the Honda Pilot I bought from Harry. I'm about to ask if she at least wants to drive around the block or something when she hands me a note.

"Here," she says.

"What's this?"

"It's for you."

I look at the piece of paper in my hand.

"You could've just sent me a text or an e-mail."

Marvel smiles. "It's not the same."

"Okay."

"Plus, I wanted you to see my cool T-shirt."

"It's pretty cool."

Marvel looks at me and smiles. There are a thousand beautiful things behind that look. A marvelous sort of ache that only a few people know about. Some miraculous sort of sorrow she's managed to walk away from.

There are a thousand things I want to say to her.

"Marvel, I—"

A gruff voice calls out her name. From a doorway, a figure stands waiting for her. It's her uncle.

"I have to go," she says.

"I know. The next time I see you will be at school."

"Will you recognize me?"

I shrug. "I don't know."

"That's okay. I'll be hanging around with a guy named Greg."

"Ooh—that's mean."

"It takes me a while to say what I want to say."

"Really?" I ask with sarcasm. "I didn't know that."

"Stop. That's why—I just wanted to say this to you. Okay?"

"Okay. Thanks."

"Marvel, right now," her uncle shouts.

Marvel smiles and turns away.

I wave in her direction one more time, then close the door.

I wonder what she's thinking. I wonder where she'll be next week. I basically can't stop thinking of this marvelous, wonderful, awesome, glorious human being.

I get back in the car and drive till I'm a block from my house, then I stop and I unfold the note.

Brandon:

FYI, I really like you.

I'll tell you a little secret. God told me to go find the most fascinating thing I could find in Appleton. So when I saw the record store, I knew. I didn't know what—or who—I'd find, but I went inside anyway. The most fascinating thing I found wasn't the boy behind the counter but the heart residing deep inside of him.

So I'll tell you another secret. I'm going to borrow that heart. Just for a while.

Be gentle with me. That's all I ask, Brandon. Especially when things get rough.

And trust me. They will get rough.

See you soon.

Marvel

73

It's late and I can't sleep. I can't do much of anything except think about her.

Maybe once school settles in, my routine and life will become normal again. Maybe this summer will be like some sweet camp experience I'll remember the rest of my life. Maybe I'm just caught up in everything, especially this girl I just met.

Maybe. But I don't think so.

Maybe Marvel is right about everything. Maybe she did hear from God and maybe she is going to do something incredible and maybe she's even going to die in the process.

In the darkness of my bedroom, I can see those eyes and that smile. They make me feel lighter and better. They bring joy and light. They're just plain good for everything. For a world full of darkness and monsters and evil.

Maybe there are monsters out there, but there are also figures standing in between, like Marvel. Sweet, mysterious Marvel. Smiling when she shouldn't smile anymore. Laughing when all she should be doing is running away. I still don't totally know this girl—she's still this dream who came over me and somehow stayed. But I like the dream. I want to stay in the dream.

Maybe I can stand in the way of those monsters, too.

ACKNOWLEDGMENTS

Thanks . . .

To Sharon, Kylie, Mackenzie, and Brianna for putting up with me.

To my parents and in-laws for constantly helping us out.

To my extended family, whom I don't see as much as I'd like to.

To Meg Wallin, for picking up The Solitary Tales and telling me how much you liked them (thus paving the way for you to acquire this series).

To L. B. Norton, for being so very L. B.–esque and making my writing better in every way.

To Claudia Cross, for staying on this writing journey with me.

To NavPress, for taking a chance on a super-big awesome bestseller like me who will break out in 2026.

To Don Pape and David C. Cook, for taking a chance on the above-mentioned teen series.

To the families who have adopted me recently: the Home Run family, the Celebrate Recovery family, the Owens family, the Masterpiece family, and the Rogers family. I love all of you guys and am thankful to be a part of your lives.

And last but not least, to Chris Buckley, who is just finishing up his first year of college and doing well. For now.

PLAYLISTS

A FASCINATION STREET PLAYLIST
1. "Dazzle" by Siouxsie and the Banshees
2. "Uncertain Smile" by The The
3. "The One Thing" by INXS
4. "Sunrise" by New Order
5. "Long Long Way to Go" by Phil Collins
6. "Perfect Girl" by The Cure
7. "Shake the Disease" by Depeche Mode
8. "Running Up That Hill" by Kate Bush
9. "Keep It Dark" by Genesis
10. "Every Little Thing She Does Is Magic" by The Police
11. "That Voice Again" by Peter Gabriel
12. "Last Night I Dreamt Somebody Loved Me" by The Smiths

A PLAYLIST FOR MARVEL
1. "Counting Stars" by OneRepublic
2. "Relentless" by Hillsong United
3. "Running to the Sea" by Röyksopp and Susanne Sundfør
4. "Hemiplegia" by HAERTS
5. "Stay Awake" by London Grammar
6. "Free at Dawn" by Small Black
7. "Mirrors" by Justin Timberlake
8. "Falling (Committed to Sparkle Motion)" by Discopolis & Axwell
9. "Denial" by I Break Horses
10. "Late Night" by Foals
11. "Bloodflood" by Alt-J
12. "Come Close Now" by Christa Wells

Another new novel from TH1NK!

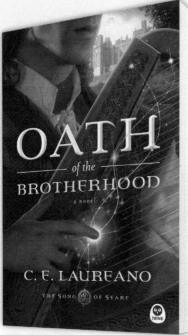

978-1-61291-587-6

OATH OF THE BROTHERHOOD

C. E. LAUREANO

In book 1 of this stunning new saga of ancient evil and
wonderworking faith, a young scholar-musician and fol-
lower of the forbidden Balian religion must discover the
power of his gifts and find the faith to pursue the path his
God has laid before him.

AVAILABLE WHEREVER BOOKS ARE SOLD.